The Macabre Collection

By David Haynes.

Cover Design by Michaela Margetts Copyright 2013

For Sarah and George.

With Special thanks to Kath Middleton.

MASK OF THE MACABRE

& OTHER
TALES OF DREAD

DAVID HAYNES

Mask of the Macabre

Contents

Mask of the Macabre

London. January 10th 1866

"To the Opera Macabre." I leapt into the Hansom and gathered my frock coat to my legs. The night was chill and an endless fall of snow had dusted my top hat entirely. The snow was a welcome sight though, for it kept the masses from the street, and in my need for haste gave the driver cause to move swiftly and without delay.

I could not remember being quite so much in anticipation, not since...Not since I had first witnessed his show in fact. When I had first observed the magician so darkly, yet beautifully enthral, beguile and with equal measure, appal me. There was a sombre grace to his act; the likes of which had never been witnessed in London before. I believed in those moments I would have done battle with Satan himself just to be in his company; to be part of the magic itself.

The cab moved quickly over the snow covered cobbles; too quickly. With every bump or turn in the road I was thrown this way and that. I thumped my cane into the roof of the cab and knocked three times; I was anxious to arrive, but to arrive in one piece I must. Tonight I was to be given the rare opportunity to meet the man himself; the magician.

I am no detective, and I am no amateur sleuth bent on revealing tricks, but it was a dark curiosity which brought me back to the theatre this night. The grim oddity of his act was as perversely captivating as spending two pennies observing the demented souls in Bethlem.

We crossed the river and entered the city. The filth, grime and toil of the working man would not be quietened even though the snow fell thick on the befouled cobbles. I looked through the window and under the smoky embrace of the gas-lit street I saw the faces of bitter men. These were the men who roared against the fell fate of their circumstance and piled their woes on our city. These were the men who would take a cut-throat to your neck for the price of a gin. One day their deeds would be accounted for, in this world or the next.

A fouler beast than those stalked the street these nights though, or so The Times reported. Some believed the devil himself was abroad and walked freely amongst our citizens. Six men had been murdered so far and all had been flayed. That is to say facially flayed and were identifiable only through their pocket watches, walking canes or trinkets of affection.

A shriek came from beyond my view and pierced the already savagely primed air. The sound, such a vile and base sound, was no doubt made during the throes of a corrupt act. I turned away. Not tonight would I debase myself and consider their blight on this city. Not tonight; tonight was for magic.

At the theatre, I alighted the cab and paid the driver, a surly man whose driving was clearly in keeping with his brusque manner. I sent him away with a reminder to be back at midnight.

"Would you kindly, sir, give me two-pence? I can get a bed to lie upon if you do, sir." I turned to see who had spoken and was greeted with a human wreck. "I shall die if I stay out another night."

She bore the traces of a past respectability in her dishevelled garments but that respectability had long since departed leaving only horrifying decay.

"I have been the victim of a terrible libertine, sir. One who sought to ruin me from the very day we met."

Her eyes were sunken wells of despair where torment swam happily among her tears. On any particular day I would have sent her away; back to the shadows where she lurked with so many others. There was something of my wife in her eyes though, my poor dead Emily, as she lay in anguish in our bed. Snatched by King Cholera himself and taken as his morbid bride. So, tonight, my spirits being what they were, I pressed four pence into her palm. With the sound of her thanks resounding through my soul I passed into The Opera Macabre once again.

Gas-lit lamps with their wine coloured shades gently illuminated the path to my box. I wanted no company tonight and would gladly have covered the cost of the theatre to sit in solitary awe. Below, in the stalls, where only last week empty seats waited for bustle and bow; barely a seat was spare. It appeared the great and the good of our society had discovered what I had already found.

The orchestra rumbled and scratched their preparation, the instruments as impatient as I for the show to commence. Then the violin began. It was as bewitchingly haunting as I recalled. The piece had remained with me all this week, weaving its tortured notes around my mind. The gas-lit chandeliers, hung high above, were faded to a hint and in the ghostly half-light cast from the wings the vivid crimson curtains became a bloody blush of velvet. The melancholy notes from the violin writhed through the theatre. They danced on the gowns of the ladies and whispered dark, dangerous thoughts into the minds of the men beside them. A noxious miasma from the gentlemen's cigars clung to the stage and I knew what was beyond that haze was equally grotesque.

Abruptly, the bass drum sounded out its deep, doom laden threat and there were gasps from several ladies as the curtains drew back.

Onto the stage he walked; the black dress tails licking at his feet like a diseased serpent's tongue. There was silence as he looked out onto the audience and folded his arms.

"Tonight ladies and gentlemen, I shall show to you the dark and duplicitous nature of man. This I will make through the many faces of the darkest magic."

His words resounded loud and clear over the crowd. They were at once, as I had been one week previously, under his thrall.

His face was as white as an alabaster trinket box and his eyes as lifeless as a memento mori photograph. As the violin played adagio, his flourishing hands gave forth a solitary crow to the void above our heads. All looked to the chandeliers as the crow circled higher and higher into the abyss. Then, when it could climb no more, it fell downwards in a sickening, screeching spiral. A bearded gentleman reached up and took the poor creature as it dropped. I smiled; as he opened his meaty fist a black silken kerchief fell to the floor and the crow was no more.

I watched the audience momentarily before averting my stare back to the magician. I believe his eyes were on me at that instant and only on me. I felt for one moment there was recognition in those inert eyes, but I must have been mistaken, for we had not yet met.

I had carefully chosen the box from which to watch him for it afforded the best vantage. His porcelain features were troubling and in his eyes nothing more than the glass beads of a doll. On his face there existed a soulless countenance, so perfectly bland and disturbing. The magician was like no man I had seen before.

The first face of duplicity he showed to the audience was that of his own mien. The transparence of his eyes shone briefly as he uttered a strange incantation in a guttural voice.

The crow, once again summoned from the smoky air, appeared and circled the magician before it dropped on him with a shrill call. Its talons scraped at his skin and ripped at his flesh until he screamed at the utter and all-encompassing agony of it. The bird flew away on glossy feathered wings and left nothing but the bloody pulp of his visage. I'd heard screams from the audience a week prior, but from my vantage, they were indecently amplified to the point of being sickening. The magician fell to his knees and clutched at his bloody face before the orchestra struck up a dirge to lament his misery.

Yet in a moment, as he stood once again, his face was repaired. Nothing but the implacable visage of an unscarred magician remained to gather the tormented applause. Where the crow had flown I could not say for the bird was of the least interest to me. Seemingly not a single talon had pulled at his flesh or marked him in any way.

For a brief moment the magician looked up and once again and I held his gaze for as long as was comfortable. His face was as porcelain pure as it had been a few moments before. Yet something slight and almost imperceptible had occurred to his features. I could not say exactly what that change was for he looked away before I could examine him further.

He took his bow and allowed the crowd to quieten before he continued.

"Our one true face is revealed in the moment of our death. Tonight I will expose my own."

The drum beat out a resounding boom. The rhythm grew faster and faster in a deafening crescendo. The magician grabbed at his chest before dropping silently to the stage. A stifled murmur rose through the crowd and the drum sounded the diminishing rhythm of his ruined heart. Then it was still. Then there was silence.

—

Almost unnoticed from the wings, crept the very vista of death. Dressed in a hooded cloak as black as midnight, and carrying his long handled scythe, he approached the supine magician.

Although I had witnessed this before, my palms were leaden with a nervous sweat which betrayed my fear. The reaper swung his great scythe down onto the magician's face sending a fountain of blood into the air. His second and third stroke finished the task and left a tattered ruin of flesh to behold. Yet the magician uttered no sound at all, not even a plea for his life. It was impossible for a man to live through such an ordeal.

The drum sounded out a beat; once, twice. Then in a steady rhythm of life it pounded the audience once again. The magician rocked upright and gazed at the spectators; his face nothing more than the rancid window of a butcher. He cried, shrieked and pleaded with the reaper beseeching him for mercy. "Give me back my life" he appeared to ask. Silence greeted his request before the weapon swept over his face and the bloody carcass fell away.

Behind it, the sickening face of Lucifer stared malevolently at the crowd. His tongue was lean, long and forked as it flicked and licked in the air and his eyes were the deepest wells of darkest ink. His mouth, in an ugly snarl, opened to speak but the reaper's scythe fell across him before he could utter a sound. In this moment his façade was renewed and he was perfect once again.

In my fervour I gripped the rail to the box and hung perilously over the balustrade. How could this be? How could a man recover from such vital injuries, not once but twice on the same night? It was not possible.

A solitary clap sounded from the shadows at the rear of the stalls. Then it was joined by another and another, until all were united together in an overture of applause. I had no doubt, many of those present felt revolted by what they had seen, as I had. As I did; but as hideous as it was something made us want more. The magician rose to his feet and took his bow, the reaper slipped silently into the shadows.

Opera Macabre was for good reason known as the 'Gloomy Boy' to those who frequented the theatres of London. The tunnels used to transport the audience to their seats were ill lit and always filled with cigar induced smog. They were, at the best of times, avoided. However on this night I was led by the usher through the tunnels to the dressing room of the magician. The usher knocked on the door and left me to wait.
I began to think the knock had gone unheard but after a few moments the door opened. I was greeted, most surprisingly, by a cheerful looking fellow. He offered his hand. "A pleasure to meet you Mr Lovett, you are most welcome." He stepped aside and beckoned me into the room.

The room was neat, tidy and although cold, felt comfortable. Two paraffin lamps lit the room and filled the air with their familiar and pleasant smell. I quickly took in my surroundings before addressing him. "It is my pleasure I can assure you Mr...?" Although he was known simply as The Magician, I did not feel it appropriate in the circumstances to address him thus.

"Sir, you may address me, Fettiplace." He tipped an ungentlemanly wink. "I should like to retain some mystery."

"As you wish sir. Your show..." I began with no real thought on how to continue. "Your show is quite remarkable. Quite, quite remarkable." Fettiplace was dressed smartly in shirt sleeves and waistcoat, although his bow tie hung carelessly around his neck. His stature, I estimated was in keeping with my own. His hair, a wild morass of silver, was the most remarkable aspect of his otherwise plain appearance.

"Thank you sir." He indicated a pair of threadbare chairs in the corner of the room. "Would you sit? I have rather a good port to drink?"

"Thank you Fettiplace. I should like that."

We sat and talked at length regarding the show and his act. He was utterly charming and quite so unalike his stage character that I had cause to question whether it was indeed, the same gentleman.

"Sir, it is my intention to create an illusion; to beguile, confuse and haunt the audience. Then of course, I endeavour to entertain them." He laughed. "These days they clamour for their amusement to be shocking."

"But Fettiplace, you are perfectly demonic on that stage, quite frightening. There is a fine line between fear and amusement sir."

"Yes Mr Lovett there is but there is also illusion. How many of us can really say our faces are an honest and truthful representation of who we really are? We slip on our mask without thought and when circumstance demands. That is all."

Fettiplace leaned forward and put me under his gaze, "You, Mr Lovett, wear a mask every day. You are wearing a mask tonight yet somewhere deep in your soul exists the real Mr Lovett. The man who would rage at what life has taken from him; yet has not the will to do so."

I looked away. For all his charm Fettiplace made me uncomfortable. Behind his head was a small door and across it lay a heavy chain and lock. It was curious and clearly too small for a man to enter. "What do you keep in there Fettiplace?"

For the first time his countenance slipped and something of the masked Lucifer re-appeared.

He half turned in his chair. "This is where my secrets are kept Mr Lovett." He turned back and smiled; his charming self once again returned. "And no, Mr Lovett, you may not peer inside."

———

I handed the empty port glass to Fettiplace and took my hat from his dresser. A lady's brooch of polished jet lay discarded on the table. The design was vaguely familiar somehow. The portrait of a beautiful young lady in profile was exquisitely crafted. Fettiplace pushed it quickly to one side, dismissively. "It has been a pleasure to talk with a gentleman such as yourself, Mr Lovett. Although I cannot guarantee any marked changes to my act, you are most welcome to visit me again, at a time of your choosing." I gave him my hand and he shook it most enthusiastically.

I bade him goodnight and walked the distance through the tunnels and out once again into the chill night. The snow had fallen thick and heavy and I began to wonder if the cab would be able, or willing to make the perilous journey. I looked about and gripped my cane tightly. Shadows moved silently in the night, especially in this district. If any footpads should chance upon me tonight they would be sorely sorry for their trouble. My cane would split their skulls as easily as a spoon cracks an egg.

To my relief, a test of strength was not needed, and as my pocket watch struck the hour, the Hansom appeared like a hearse through the mist.

I lay in my bed that night and wondered about the curious magician, Mr Fettiplace. A man, so demonic and abominable on stage, was a jolly and sociable fellow with scarce a bad word for any man. A strange juxtaposition, make no mistake. But his cheery manner had been disrupted at the mention of the strange little doorway. What manner of secrets did he keep locked away in there? I suppose, if I were a man of magic, and someone tried to reveal my secrets, I too might become irritable.

I took breakfast promptly at nine. I had a great number of visits planned for the morning and would benefit from the early start. The front page of The Times was once gain filled with the night's grisly atrocities. Another three bodies had been found and each one suffered the same facial disfigurement. There was speculation about the motive for such an act.

The editor clearly apportioned the deeds to a vigilante group of prostitutes cutting through their brutal customers. I could not align myself with this thinking. Women were simply not capable of such barbarous acts, not even the filthy creatures in their brothels.

My first visit of the day was to be to the offices of The Athenaeum. The journal frequently published my reviews of the latest literary works and I was keen to show them my most recent examination. I found Lewis Carrol's book 'Alice's Adventures in Wonderland.' to be almost without rival in its preaching of nonsense. The book so infuriated me that, should it not have cost such a princely sum, I would happily have seen it on the bed of The Thames.

With high spirits I left my home. The heavy snow fall of the previous evening should have left the streets clean and sparkling in the winter sun. Instead a mist clung to the street and draped the gas lights in an ill-fitting robe. Finding a Hansom would be problematic and I decided it would be a perfect morning to walk the short distance.

My spirits were disturbed shortly after leaving though, for with an odious sensation I began to feel watched. Pausing and gazing about, I could see no obvious signs of this, but the feeling was with me and it left me uncomfortable. With each step I felt scrutinised and examined. I imagined I could hear the crisp sound of a footfall landing in step with mine.

I had all but convinced myself it was nothing more than an uneasy mood which had taken grip, most probably caused by the gruesome show of the night before. Then I saw her. Across the street, in the arboretum, I glanced upon a lady looking over at me with something in her hand. Her crimson dress was as startling as a droplet of freshly spilled blood against the snow. I stopped and our eyes met. For a second she seemed oblivious to our role reversal, but when she realised, she slipped the article into her purse. What was it? A pencil, some paper perhaps?

She turned and walked quickly away; nothing more than a crimson spectre against the threadbare, frosted trees. You would ask; why did Lovett not follow and enquire into the lady's purpose? I would ask that too but in the moment I felt shaken. I suspected I knew the lady and our paths had crossed before.

I had been a little too fond of the Limehouse district and the tincture of opium in my early years. Something my father had been keen to supress. My dear wife had finally driven it from my system once we were married but not before scandal had threatened. A great deal of my father's money had been spent to assuage the furore. Yet, like the tendrils of some long forgotten opium induced dream, the threads of a memory twisted amid my wits. Was this apparition someone from the past?

Following a brief but satisfactory conversation with the editor of The Athenaeum, I decided my nerves required a little help to settle. Unable to conduct my remaining business I took lunch at the club. The chill atmosphere of the street was at once removed as I stepped inside the welcoming and warm interior. My usual comrades had not yet arrived; their business was clearly greater than my own.

I settled at my usual place beside the fire and once again picked up a copy of The Times. Aside from the price of stock and Lord Derby's proposed political reforms, there was little of note. This only served to bring me back to the ghoulish events of the last few nights.

The deceased men had all been scalped; their faces removed exposing the sinew beneath. What diseased state of mind would drive a man to commit such an act? To take another man's face and… and do what exactly?

I left the club a little before four, having discussed the matter at length with acquaintances both familiar and unfamiliar. Whatever theoretical nonsense they expounded upon always brought me back to the same resolve. I did not reveal my thoughts to them for fear of ridicule but they remained to the forefront of my theory. Although Fettiplace had, by all standards, appeared as unremarkable as any other man; I was convinced his macabre masks had a part to play.

The snow had fallen heavily again and finding the relative warmth of a Hansom would be difficult not to say dangerous on such an evening.

"…you are most welcome to visit me again, at a time of your choosing." Fettiplace's words rang in my ears. I was some distance from both home and Opera Macabre but it seemed certain that I would find answers in the Gloomy Boy and not beside the warm fireside at home.

Through the ragged gas-lit streets of London I trudged, feeling the cold stares of the depraved beasts as I passed their lairs. Twice I was accosted by haunted creatures imploring me for money. I gave the first woman two pennies for a bed and sent her away with little hope she would not use it for gin. The second, a man of stout build, coughed his way through a declaration of imminent death. The foul stench of gin was already on his breath and I sent him away with a bruise from my cane.

Eventually I found myself at the very point where the Hansom had delivered me the night before. I dared not think that Fettiplace would be here, for it was too early, and for this I was thankful. I had already decided on a course of action and judging by his reaction when I mentioned his secret locker; that course would not be at all welcome.

Dressed as I was, it was of little concern to the usher that I be allowed access to the tunnels and to the dressing room of the magician. I was after all a gentleman, beyond reproach.

The Gloomy Boy was, if at all possible, gloomier than when heaving with the bodies of Victorian society. The inadequate gas lights threw my shadow like a twisted monster along the curved walls. As I walked those dark passageways towards the magician's room I felt as a collier must feel on his way to the face; depressed and alone.

Thankfully, for my legs were unaccustomed to the exertions of such lengthy exercise, the distance was short. Before many minutes had passed I was outside his room again.

I rapped on the door with my cane and waited. I rapped again before entering.

"Fettiplace?" I called, expecting no reply.

As I had hoped the room was empty save for stage attire, which lay inside his portmanteau. A single paraffin lamp had been lit in preparation for his arrival.

I checked my pocket watch. It was approaching six and the show was due to begin at seven. There would not be much time to complete my task.

His secret door in the corner was once again secured with a chain. Rattle it as I could, it could not to be opened. I searched his dressing table for keys but there were none and just as I began to feel at a loss a voice came from behind.

"Sir, may I enquire as to your purpose?"

I froze, excuses already racing through my head. Slowly, I turned and opened my mouth to speak. A fear took hold as soon as I saw who had addressed me.

"Sir, I ask again, why are you here?"

It was the foul creature I had given pennies to the previous night. Her vapid expression had gone, replaced with a determined mien I had not expected.

I quickly gathered my thoughts. "I may ask of you, the same madam, are we not both out of place here?" I reached into my waistcoat for a penny to send her away.

"You may not buy me with a penny sir, not today." She toyed with the brooch at her breast, the black contrasted against the bright crimson of the silk…

"I have seen you before, in the arboretum today. You were watching me."

She smiled; an unpleasant sight in the gloom. "Do you not recognise me Jonathan? Have you forgotten these eyes? You once told me they were your opium. Your laudanum and all the dreams you ever wished for."

At once, a distant opium filled revelation came swirling into my mind. It was of a woman of beauty and of grace who I had beguiled and defiled. She was that woman.

"My father paid you." I uttered.

"But the child lived on Jonathan. It lived on in my belly and grew twisted and bent like a fiend in a nightmare. Then when they dragged it screaming from my womb it was thrown on the pyre like a dead cat." Her words were uttered with spiteful vengeance.

"I will pay Susanna. I will pay to put things straight. I have changed."

She held up her hand, to quieten my offer. "It is not your money we want Jonathan. It is your life."

"We?" I asked. Who was she in league with?

Susanna smiled and removed a scrap of paper from her purse, "My brother and I." She turned the paper and showed me a sketch. "Do you recognise this man Jonathan?"

I stepped closer. The sketch was of me. "It appears to be me."

"Yes it is and you have the deceitful face of a murderer." She tucked the paper back into her purse.

—

17

This conversation had gone on for too long and was as distasteful as it was unexpected. I did not understand the purpose of the sketch other than to taunt me. "I shall leave now but you know where to find me if my offer is to your taste." I made to walk past her, all thoughts of Fettiplace and his dark magic behind me. Susanna, it appeared, was not quite finished.

"You ruined me!" she shrieked and raised her hand to strike me. It was neither with intention nor force that I struck her with the ivory handle of my cane. But strike her I did and she fell clumsily to the floor.

This was an unfortunate accident and one which was beyond my expertise to repair. I knelt and checked her pulse. It beat strongly like the thump of a drum in an orchestra. She had been so beautiful once; so young and beautiful and it was my cowardice that had ruined her. I ran my fingers softly across her cheek. In different times Susanna.

The black brooch had fallen from her breast onto the floor and I picked it up to look at the work; but something in the brooch was wrong. For all the dark beauty it possessed, it was too heavy for its size. I turned it in my fingers and a small clasp dropped from the back releasing a small silver key.

In an instant I forgot about poor Susanna and unlocked the chain from Fettiplace's secret store. I could not enter the room for the malevolent stench which immediately pervaded the air was as vile as death itself. I could not see in either for the blanket of darkness which filled the space was complete.
I grabbed the lamp and thrust it into the unending darkness. For a moment the shadows were unyielding, crowding the light and forcing it back. But the light grew in strength and forced the shadows away until the room was illuminated in a flickering gloom.

On the walls were the faces of slaughtered men. Their cadaverous masks hung like hunting prizes on a country estate, but these trophies were not to be admired. These were made to be worn. Where once lived eyes were vapid orbs of loss and despair. I turned away, already feeling the acid bile rising in my throat.

Fettiplace was as debauched as his show suggested and his true face had been revealed in hideous clarity. His stage masks were indeed the real flesh of butchered men. I needed to be free of this morbid mausoleum and bring a constable to witness this atrocity.

"Sir, there's nothing in here, bar a pig's head. It's pretty ripe though I'll give you that." The constable had been difficult to find but had come immediately seeing my distress.

"That cannot be. I saw the men's faces carved and hung like trophies."

"Have a look for yourself, sir." The constable handed me the lamp and I peered inside. It was an empty space, no sign of the macabre masks.

A crowd had gathered about the theatre, the show had been cancelled and no sign of Fettiplace or Susanna could be found.

The constable accompanied me home, fearing I was deluded and liable to cause injury to another. His intentions were kindly enough but I did not doubt what I had seen. One does not easily forget the spectacle of what was in that room. I took a bottle of brandy to my room and lay clothed on the bed. I knew that sleep would not come and the chimes of a bell from a distant church counted out a tortuous route to dawn. A cold depression had gripped me during the night hours but I resolved to speak with the police again and implore them to investigate.

The bell chimed eight times and I rose from the bed. The first of the grey morning light staggered through the bedroom window barely illuminating my steps. I peered outside and looked to the street below.

A cab was parked beneath my window. I was not expecting visitors, least of all at this hour. The door to the cab opened and out flowed a river of crimson silk. Susanna looked up and waved happily. It was a curiously friendly gesture and for a moment I was in a mind to wave back. Fettiplace appeared at her side and bowed before tipping his top hat and returning to the warmth of the cab. Had this all been a cruel joke? Was I the source for his amusement?

I would have my answers this day. Taking two steps at a time I descended the stairs at a dangerous speed and out onto the street. The cab had gone from view but I ran in the direction it must have taken. The snow lay underfoot and my feet were bare sending me sprawling into the snow. Finally, cursing I got to my feet, and stepped back inside. My resolve, had it not been firmly set was now cast in stone. I would find Fettiplace and wring his putrid neck.

I picked up The Times from beneath the door and observed the headline, "Four Men Slain."
So the killer had been busy again, slicing his way through the city. If Fettiplace was indeed responsible then they would see him hang, of that there could be no doubt. It was my desire to see him treated so.

"Killer identified."
My heart stopped beating. Beneath the headline was a picture of me, an artist had sketched my face on the front of the paper.

"Killer identified."
I staggered into the dining room, gasping for air. I had killed no man and yet here I was. "Killer witnessed in the act."

The floor beneath my feet seemed to swell with each step and threatened to trip me. I grasped for the table and where my hands expected wood they found something else. With a sickening dread I looked to my fingers. Beneath my hand was a bloody mask cut from the flesh of men. My fingers slipped through the voids where once lived eyes and lifted it to my face. The mask had been cut seamlessly, flawlessly and with the touch of an artist. Between them they had created the perfect countenance of Jonathan Lovett; and in doing so had made me the murderer.

Doctor Harvey

Bethlem Lunatic Asylum.
London 1868

Allow me to introduce myself. I am Doctor Harvey. The name would suggest an affiliation with all matters medical and whilst this is correct, I have to point out that I am neither a Doctor, nor qualified in any medical field whatsoever. My name is Doctor Harvey.

My father named me thus in honour of his uncle; Doctor William Harvey. He was both a qualified and practising man of medicine. Such was my father's admiration for this man that I became a demonstration of that respect. The record of my birth shows that on the 8th of March 1823 Doctor Harvey Lightfoot was born into this world. The son of Louisa Lightfoot (nee Meeks) and Henry Lightfoot (Clerk).

Early in my life the name gave rise to much confusion amongst my peers. They could not fathom, especially on first introduction, that I was in fact not a man of medicine. Understandably, for a short period I began to introduce myself not as Doctor Harvey but as Harvey Lightfoot; a simple name, unlikely to cause confusion.

However, I found quite quickly that this name, although less confusing, garnered a good measure less respect from those I met.

Not being blessed with the brains or connections to pursue a career in medicine was an unfortunate genetic comedy of sorts. However I found I had something infinitely superior to the wit and affiliates required. I discovered I was a confident actor of superior but deceitful quality.

I had long been a customer of the dollymops and common prostitutes in the east end, something I kept from my father's accounts. But one evening as I hurried along the Ratcliffe Highway, and hurry I did, for that district is rife with extreme violence and murder; I happened across a prone woman lying injured on the street.

It was not unheard of for men to fall foul of this subterfuge, to stop and offer assistance only to be waylaid and beaten in one of the alleyways, their belongings stolen. There was something of this woman though, something which told me she was not merely acting. Flashily dressed with dirty feathers hanging from her bonnet she lay on the wet cobbles with not a care for her attire. It was not in my nature to be so callous a man as to leave her in this state, so I knelt and felt her neck.

"Will she live Doctor?" A feminine voice asked from over my shoulder.

I turned, about to utter the words I'd been saying since I was a child. 'I'm not a Doctor.' But I checked my response. I may not have held the surgeon's bag or knife but to this lady I was such a man.

"Lizzie's been felled!" She called out and like rats from a lair, the unclean vagabonds spilled out from their seedy holes and gathered about.

Lizzie displayed a red mark to her forehead. Through drink or otherwise, she had clearly fallen. "She needs to lie flat in the warm and be given a tincture. Her health will return."

A brute of a man gathered her in his arms and carried her back to the shadows from where she had come. I felt a touch on my arm.

"Thank you Doctor; will you step inside and allow the girls to show you their thanks?" I looked at the gathered faces of the crowd. They were all women; gaudily dressed in their frilly fineries and ready for work. I had, as luck may have it, found one of their own.

"I should be happy to be recompensed in such a way."

23

And there in the rapture of sex was my medical career conceived.

For many years I treated the denizens of that foul district as their one and only Doctor. They could not well afford the expensive remedies prescribed by others but I provided a service both efficient and in the main, effective.

I was happy for a while and in payment for my service to the ladies I was provided lodgings, a pint of brandy and food each day. There were some unfortunate slips when a surgical hand was required, but by and by, I was well liked and well used.

It was perhaps with some inevitability that one of my peers, Staniforth came to use the brothel where I kept my lodgings. His surprise at seeing me after so long was only rivalled by the look of surprise when he learned of my role.

"A Doctor? You are no more a physician than I a prince." He laughed loud. "I shall enjoy telling the others of this. Everyone shall know of Doctor Harvey the fool."

It wasn't the others I was afraid of or their derision; it was the fury of the vicious cats who worked in the brothel and their brutal protectors.

I had only felt another man's windpipe when observing a pulse; feeling the steady, strong flow of blood beneath his skin. Yet, Staniforth soon had my hands on his throat for the opposite means. The crushing of his windpipe brought with it the wrath of the middle classes. In the blink of an eye, a purge began, and the unfortunate creatures they sought to protect were driven out of the brothels and onto the street.

I do not recall what became of me during my months of exile. I wandered as a festering creature, devoid of hope, for a murderer's soul cannot be saved. My false medical career was all I had left, my one way to offer atonement for my sin. For a deeper and darker sin cannot be committed.

The medicine of the mind had never been of much interest to me. However with the situation as it was and my desperate need to atone, I found myself at Bethlem. It was here that I met a curious individual named Jonathan Lovett.

It was by some miracle that neither Lovett nor I had been hanged for our crimes but instead both incarcerated in the asylum; one as Doctor, one as patient. During his spree of the most foul and degrading murder I had been, at large, in a blithe torpor. The fact remained he had almost certainly slaughtered ten men. What magic or rather, expense had kept him from the gallows was of little concern but in the correct place, he most certainly was. We both were.

He was of course, kept in a cell on the second floor, and chained to the wall like so many others. And like so many others he screamed and wailed at the cause of his downfall. In Lovett's case it was the name Fettiplace he muttered, uttered and cursed throughout his waking and dreaming hours.

The hopeless entreaties to the unseen figures who sat in their minds echoed along the dim galleries of the hospital. A dark and mournful dirge sung by a lunatic cast.

Lovett was not treated for his condition, for what treatment could possibly bring him back to the realms of supposed normality? He was however given an almost unprecedented amount of attention by London society. The gentlemen, and surprisingly ladies, paid two pennies to come and observe him, and of course, the other miserable wretches in our care. It was, for them at least, a demented melodrama performed by a grotesque troupe; but amuse them it did. As utterly abhorrent as this was, the financial rewards could not be underestimated so the matinees continued.

Lovett's case provoked a curiosity in me which I was unable to shake. Whether it was the macabre nature of his actions or the eloquence of his voice, I cannot say; but I took to standing outside his cell, heeding his rants.

"Masks, hundreds of them hung on the wall. Hundreds I tell you, hundreds!"

"Where is Fettiplace? Bring him to me and I shall rip his mask and show you his true face!"

"Bring me my mask so I may show you!"

My enquiries told me, this mask of which Lovett spoke, was discovered at his home when he was arrested. He wore it as the officers took hold of him and fought to keep it in place. At his trial it was found to contain the flesh of at least six men, perhaps more. What dire mind had this creature been afflicted with? Delusions and manias were in the very spirit of these men and no man can see his own delusion particularly if he is at the root of it.

I took to delivering his molasses sweetened gruel personally and watching him for a while. Chained at the neck and utterly filthy he clung to the wall of his putrid cell like a frightened animal. His eyes never left mine, not once.

"You, Doctor Harvey are wearing a mask, are you not?" Lovett's face bore the signs of scratches and scars where his fingers had clawed at his flesh.

"A mask Lovett? No, not I." I took hold of my flabby cheeks to illustrate the point.

"But you are, Doctor Harvey, I can see it under your skin; just below the surface." He smiled; a grim and soulless leer which left me cold.

Lovett was a lunatic, of that there was no question, but his manner, so calm and measured in conversation left me uneasy.

Back in my room I wrote up my notes, for even an acting physician must have papers. I simply substituted the names of the patients on the older reports from my predecessor, for were they not all the same?

The doctor's room was scarce any larger than Lovett's cell, and although there was a desk and comfortable bed, the room was a cheerless and desperate place. I was thankful it was beside the quieter patients on the first floor. The miserable screams of Lovett and the others on the floor above was but a distant and ghostly echo.

For the next few days, Lovett and I conversed daily, and I began to spend more and more time in his company. For all his eloquence and intelligence, his obsession with Fettiplace and his macabre masks was never far from his thoughts. They were both literal and figurative but real to him in equal measure. I could not remove the chains from his neck but I could at least try and remove them from his soul.

That is not to say, all was well with Lovett, for the longer we spoke about the horrifying masks the more agitated he became.

"I'll show you what lies beneath!" He shrieked and dug down into his hollowed cheeks and opened a trench. Such was his desire to mutilate himself that it took four men to restrain him. What lay beneath his skin was nothing more than what lay beneath all our flesh; blood and bones. But Lovett was convinced something more than that lay beneath and try as I might I could not convince him otherwise.

"What mask do you wear, Doctor Harvey?" Lovett asked.

"I wear no mask, I am simply Doctor Harvey and that is all." I replied.

"But is not Doctor Harvey a faceted man? Are you unflawed, without blame or fault? I do not believe such a man exists." Lovett peered at me, diverting his eyes to my cheek. "You have an injury, Doctor Harvey, your cheek is bleeding."

I touched my face and gazed at my finger. A smudge of blood adorned its tip. "A shaving cut no doubt, Lovett."

"Yes quite."

I took my leave and made my way down to the first floor, past the never ending cries of tormented souls and the stench of their waste. A single spot of blood had dried on my cheek leaving a scarlet mole where none had been before. I dabbed it away and fell on my bed.

Lovett and his damn masks were infuriating. The echo of his madness swept along the gallery and fell on my room. I began to wonder if he would not benefit from a visit to the filthy tiles of the treatment table.

I awoke early the next morning. In Bethlem, the morning chorus is not the sweet song of a lark. It is the screaming howl of a waking nightmare from a resident. The refrain was as familiar and unremarkable to me as the cries of the hawkers at Covent Garden are to the common man. My thoughts returned, as was often the case these mornings, to Lovett. There were no treatments for a man such as he, save for the collar and chain. His days of disfiguring and torturing innocent people had finished. Yet, he possessed a peculiar charm which made me consider my own position.

The skin on my face itched with the night's growth, but as I rubbed my face, I felt the stinging sensation of an open wound. The nerve endings twitched through my skin and jolted me from my Lovett reverie; shocking me from my bed. I looked to my hands and saw the creases lined with blood. There was no great amount, but enough to paint a crimson disguise. I must have scratched myself in the night with a loose and jagged fingernail.

I washed, dressed and left my room. I was determined to speak with Lovett again and to convince him of his need to remove this Fettiplace from his mind; to accept that whatever masks he had seen were those of a theatrical nature and nothing more.

I arrived on the upper floor and walked the distance along the gallery to Lovett's cell. A thin and despairing light fell from the windows, perfectly matched with my mood. I had all but stemmed the drops of blood from the mark to my face, but as I reached for the door, a solitary drop landed on my hand. It congealed in an instant and I wiped it away.

In the half-light of his grim lodgings I spied a great pool of black liquid beside his cot. I need not enter to see it was blood, Lovett's blood. But what had become of this poor tormented soul?

I took the gallery stairs at pace for there were only two places Lovett could be. The infirmary or the mortuary and I prayed it was the former. A great scream of despair rose from one of the cells as I passed but I dared not stop to observe the source.

I had scarce been in the infirmary, but in contrast to the rest of the hospital, the walls were clean and brightly tiled in the most vivid white imaginable. Imprisoned, like the rest of the souls in Bethlem, a single golden canary sat lonely in his cage by the door. His cheerful little song was unable to change my disposition.

Were it not for the board above his bed, I would not have recognised him, such were his injuries. He lay in the only occupied berth, at the far end of the room, beneath a small window overlooking the inner courtyard.

"Lovett, who has done this to you?" I asked although I knew the answer. He did not reply. His face, if that is what was left, was nothing more than a gruesome vista of meat. The wound wept slowly onto the already soiled sheets. He had finally done what he so badly wanted. He had shown me a monster existed beneath his flesh.

He opened his lips to speak, the flash of pain evident through his eyes, but no sound came.

"What is it Lovett? What do you want to tell me?" I fought back the revulsion and put my head close to his mouth.

"The monster is not here, he has flown." His voice croaked.

"There was never one there Lovett, only in your mind you poor demented soul." I spoke softly.

"I never killed those men. It was Fettiplace."

My flesh crawled as I stared into those weeping eyes. "Be still." It was all I could say. "Be still Lovett."

Before I could pull away he reached out a hand and took my arm. "You have given much of your time making me see the monster for what he really is. Now let me aid you. Look to your own mask. Look to your room and see what is real and what is not." He fell back; the effort clearly too great to continue.

The utterances of a lunatic in his death throes would not normally trouble me so; but Lovett had invaded my mind and something resonated inside. 'Look to your own mask.'

It was the mask of a fabricated Doctor in an asylum for lunatics; that is what it was. I wandered back to my room, pausing at Lovett's obscene den, and peered inside. Unseen in my earlier haste, pieces of flesh littered the grimy floor, like birdseed for doves in the park. "Poor Lovett" I whispered into the void. I could stand the sight no longer for I felt suddenly nauseous and hurried to my room.

'Look to your own mask. Look to your room and see what is real.' A drop of fresh blood fell to the floor beside my desk. It was true my room was little more than a cell, a small square cell. But a warm rug lay across the cold floor beside my bed. Look, there it…Where was the rug?

Drip, drop.

And where are my desk and patient reports? This infernal scratch on my cheek is unrelenting. I cannot soothe it away.

Drip, drip, drop.

My hands around Staniforth's scrawny neck and the last of his breath on my cheek. A billy club cracked on my skull

Drip, drip, drop drop.

So much blood on the floor. A chain beside the bed, a neck collar. Am I the patient? No, it cannot be, I am Doctor Harvey.

"Fetch a nurse!" A voice in the gallery. "Fetch the nurse!"

Hands on my arms, grabbing my hands but I must free them. I am no patient. They must see that. I must show them. Beneath this mask is my true face; beneath the mask is Doctor Harvey.

"I am beneath the mask! Look beneath the mask!" I can feel my fingers beneath the skin; brushing against the bone and muscle then ripping it off. Rip it all off.

"I am Doctor Harvey!"

"Be still Doctor Harvey." A soft voice in my ear. "Be still, or you will find your lodgings on the second floor, once again."

Memento Mori

The first occasion I observed a corpse, I was beside the bed of my deceased father. Perfectly still, yet only seconds prior, he had been gripped by a hideous convulsion which threatened to break him in half. There, under the stained and bloody sheets, I looked for the final time upon the lifeless body of my progenitor. I was not frightened and I was not grief-stricken, for I felt that his body had been released from the terrible pain it had long endured. Amid the wailing sound of my mother's misery I gazed at his face and tried not to forget.

In the moments that passed, his body was covered with the soiled sheets, and taken away. As to where it was taken, I did not know, but I remained where I was and closed my eyes. I kept the image of him in my mind for as long as I could.

Memories are fleeting, some more than others, but none is eternally exact. We embellish and decorate our reminiscences with elegant mendacities where our wits fail to recall. This is humanity, and some may say, it is a failing in our creation.

The image of my father's body remained with me for as long as it took me to pass through puberty. After that, he was merely an indistinct figure, present only in my dreams.

A cologne bottle stands empty on my dresser, the last drops long since gone. The faintest of his scent still lingers on the stopper and reminds me of him. It won't be long before the trace is entirely departed; like the sound of his voice and the touch of his gruff, calloused hand, lamented so long ago.

This yearned for loss of memory led me to my current profession as a photographer. For many years I completed an apprenticeship under the experienced guidance of Mr. Saundersfoot, who apart from being a competent photographer, was a skilled teacher. His studio, modest by some standards, was always well used and popular, if not necessarily with the class of society he had hoped to attract. Saundersfoot taught the basics of the craft, but his ambitions were, at least to me, infuriatingly humble.

"We must cater to the tastes of the masses now, Richard. Photography is not an art; It is merely a function which we use to help us remember." That function is exactly the reason why I adore this profession.

Saundersfoot passed, and without an heir, I took his studio as my own. Fashions change like the passage of the seasons and photography was no different. The stilted images of grim faced families sitting precisely on the posing couch were no longer in demand. My training under Saundersfoot, as comprehensive, as it had been, was deliberately conservative. It had focused entirely on capturing the grim faced stoicism of the common man and nothing more adventurous. As a result of this dogmatism, and whilst under my care, W.A. Saundersfoot (Photographer) almost became a financial ruin. I take my share of the blame for that but, had Saundersfoot been alive, the result would have been the same.

It was because this threat that I made the decision to widen the appeal of the studio. For some time I had admired the trick photography done by men far more skilled than I. A headless man with his face served on a salver was a particular favourite. It was with regret that I realised I was unable to produce such wonderful images.

So, for all his inflexibility, Saundersfoot's stoic resistance to change gave me the necessary training to become one of London's finest exponents in the art of Memento Mori. The taste for 'Remember your mortality' photography amongst the whole of society was almost an overnight phenomenon. It provided others with something I would never have; an exact recollection of their loved ones in death.

You may find this somewhat distasteful, and indeed, when my first assignment came I found it an arduous task. As they say though, money is money, and when that commodity is in short supply, it is sometimes necessary to do tasks against which your soul rebels.

My first assignment was a simple task. Yet, as it was my first, it forever remains with me. A girl of twenty years had been taken by consumption. In life, no doubt, she had been pretty with a ruddy complexion but in death, as one would expect, her features were wan. Since the death of my father, this was the first corpse I had seen. If it had not been for the weary look in their grief stricken eyes I am ashamed to say my revulsion would have been obvious.

Nevertheless, I remained professional, and photograph her I did. There were three beating hearts and one stopped for eternity gathered in the little parlour of their home as I arranged my equipment.

Dressed in a black silken gown with a string of pearls hung around her neck, she was propped between her parents. Her eyes were closed as they had been in her dying moments and were left so; after all she was merely sleeping to them. Her mother grasped her daughter's stiffened hand and wailed briefly before her husband brushed away her tears. I cannot stand to think what this loss did to their lives and what became of them after the photograph was taken. In my mind I hope it provided a small amount of comfort. My wish was that they could look upon their daughter everyday, as I was not able to with my father.

34

I will not trivialise the matter with talk regarding the technical aspect of photography. Suffice it to say, it is nothing more than a gruesome scientific joke, that in memento mori the living becomes the ghost. The very tranquillity possessed by cadavers negates the lengthy exposure the image requires. In contrast, the living cannot be still for even a moment. The beat of our heart and the blood in our veins send silent messages to our nerves; like a shudder in the cold or a flinch from the debauched touch of a corpse's hand. It is in the instant that they move that their image becomes a ghostly blur on the copy.

It was not always the case that I was called to photograph the dead. I have, on many occasions, been called to record an image premortem. That is to say, in the moments where all hope is gone, I am called to record their image forever more. It has often been the case where I wait in the shadow of some darkened room until the priest has said his piece. Then, like the reaper himself, I come to take their soul. It is no different, for they say at the moment of death our souls can go anywhere they choose and why not the lens of my camera? It is I though, and not the reaper, who leave a living image behind and not some faded memory of what went before.

The images I leave behind record the moment perfectly. Unlike my brain which fails to recall much at all. So, with that in my mind, I will not attempt to recollect any more of the appointments I've been given. Besides, it may be considered in bad taste to reveal very much more.

This précis of my career brings me to this point and the story I now wish to tell. For, although I am well used to being in the company of the dead, and as you have heard, recording their image. My most recent assignment was unalike any other I had previously taken and left me disturbed.

I received a call at my studio one morning from a well presented, and clearly, affluent gentleman. His entrance, however, was far less elegant than his attire. Such was his haste that he tripped on the stoop as he entered, almost falling to the floor.

He removed his top hat. "Sir, I am Rowland Eldritch from Eldritch and Maypole, solicitors at law. You may have heard of us?"

"I'm afraid not Mr Eldritch. Fortunately I have had little use for legal matters thus far. What service may I be, sir?"

Eldritch assumed a distinct look of disappointment to his flabby face. It was clear his reputation was of great importance to him. "You are Saundersfoot I presume?"

"No sir, I am Richard..." Eldritch held up his gloved hand. My name was obviously unimportant.

"I have come to request your services."

I took up my ledger and made preparations to record the details. "And who are you acting on behalf of Mr Eldritch?"

"Acting for?" He had momentarily been distracted by the display of my work.

I tapped my ledger. "Yes sir. Who shall I record as the client?"

He peered closely at a photograph of a poor deceased infant wrapped in her christening gown. "These photographs are particularly disturbing." He removed a white handkerchief and dabbed at his mouth. He clearly found the material distasteful.

"Sir?" I enquired again.

"Yes?" He turned away from the image with a look of disgust on his face. "The name? You do not need to know the name." He handed me a card adorned with an address. "My client does not wish to be named but you are requested at the address precisely at eight o'clock this evening."

I took the card from him. "My rate sir is..."

Eldritch turned away as if the discussion of finance was as distasteful as the image of the infant. "I have been instructed to pay double your usual rate. I suggest you accept the offer."

I need not think about such an offer, for although business was good, there was no telling when the boom would end. "Gladly I'll accept it sir. You may tell your client I shall arrive promptly at eight."

Eldritch said no more and walked from the studio as quickly as he could without running. Photography, I suspected, was not to his taste; particularly photography of the dead.

I turned the card over in my hand. It was simple yet with an elegance to the writing which suggested wealth. Indeed, being paid so handsomely for what was my usual business indicated a strong desire in addition to fortune. I put the excessive payment down to the urgent nature of the request and gave the matter no more thought.

I arrived at the address, as instructed, promptly at eight and gave the driver a penny to aid me with my equipment. I knew from the card that the address was on a fashionable and expensive avenue in Belgravia; and had Saundersfoot still been alive, he would have clapped both hands together at his good fortune. This was the abode of a family of considerable wealth. I took the steps and the door and knocked three times. Attached to the door was wreath of laurel, tied with black ribbon. It warned of a death within.

A servant allowed me entrance and led me, in silence, along a gloomy corridor. In the flickering light of the spluttering gas lamps I spied portraits hung on the wall. As soon as the vague image of one faded away, so began the frame of another. I could not hope to count them all, for not a bare space of wall was to be found. The members of this family were all recorded on canvas in oil; but none was as exact as a photograph taken by me.

In the hall I was presented by a valet who, taking some of my equipment, led me in silence up the stairs to the second floor. The picture was no less gloomy for although the portraits had gone, they had been replaced by faded and tattered tapestries. In the passing of a loved one you may expect the mood to be black, yet flowers are often placed to brighten the tone. In this house no such attempt had been made. The chill atmosphere of the house was both literal and symbolic and a shiver danced swiftly along my spine.

The valet led me to the front of the house and into the drawing room. Immediately the mood changed. A fire had been lit and raged noisily in the hearth, sending crackling shadows all about the room. I was greeted by a tall gentleman of advanced years. He immediately took my hand. "Sir, I am glad you have come. Will you take a brandy before we begin?" He indicated for the valet to wait.

"I should like that very much sir. How may I address you? Your man failed to introduce me." His frail hand gripped mine with a bony embrace. The man was gaunt, almost skeletal, and I suspected whatever expression he chose to wear would present an unpleasant visage. An oversized suit hung from his frame like a filthy coal sack.

"I am Matthew, simply Matthew."

I looked about the room. Whatever decadence this room had seen in the past was now long forgotten. Ragged drapes clung to the windows; their threadbare filaments were like tangled webs.

"Would you sit for a moment?" Matthew indicated a sofa beside the fire and the valet placed a crystal glass in my hand.

The sofa had been well used and whatever upholstery remained was like medieval torture instruments along my back.

Matthew took his position beside the fireplace and put his hand upon the lid of a black urn. "I expect you are wondering why I have paid you twice your usual amount to conduct this assignment."

"Sir, it is not my place to wonder. I have come at short notice and that is enough for me."

Matthew laughed; a cold and miserable sound. "Very good, but I shall tell you a little of the matter before us. I have seen your eyes upon my house; the signs of decay and loss are evident." He tapped the lid of the urn. "My wife is long gone but she would despair at what has become of us. As you can see we were a wealthy family but neither time nor fortune has been our friend. There have been... indiscretions which have taken considerable portions of that wealth and there have been more recent incidents which have taken my health. I know I am not long for this plane."

Matthew, appeared ill, of that there was no doubt. If this was to be my assignment, then so be it, although it appeared somewhat premature.

"You have finished your brandy sir?" Matthew asked and I handed the glass to the valet.

Matthew took the urn of his wife's ashes and walked towards the drawing room door. "Shall we begin then?"
The valet took my equipment and we both followed Matthew back out into the cold passage. Should one miscreant spark from the spluttering lamp land on the dusty old tapestries I had no doubt we would all be cremated in an instant. Matthew's pace was slow and deliberate, but considering his frame, this was unsurprising.

Eventually we reached a closed door. "Let us begin then." He pushed open the door and stepped inside.

As I have told before, I am well used to houses where death has a room of its own. Even with that experience, there was nothing which could prepare me for the foul, malevolent stench of decay which greeted my passage into that room. I swallowed the sour taste of brandy as it warmed my throat on the way back out of my gut.

On every surface there stood jugs of decaying lilies, their petals drooping and brown. Whatever perfume their delicacy once possessed was now absorbed in the reek of mortis. I was thankful no fire had been lit in the room, for although the biting chill of the air was uncomfortable, I had no doubt the heat would have amplified the reek.

A single high backed sofa was turned away to face the empty fireplace; there were no other items of furniture present. Above the hearth, an enormous elaborate mirror was hung and in the oppressive gloom I could see a gossamer veil had been draped upon it.

I could see no body; but the smell told my senses one was present. It was undoubtedly lying in the dark, hidden from view.

"My son lies there." Matthew's bony finger, like a diseased twig, pointed to the sofa.

With some dread I approached the settee; it was uncommon for a body to hold such a reek as this. At no other residence had I gone beyond a four day wake; I suspected this had been longer.

Lying full length on the settee was the body of a man. He was dressed, as was the custom, in an evening suit. Neither the valet nor Matthew had come any closer to the sofa and I now stood and alone in the gloom. It was impossible to see any further detail.

"I shall need more light sir; without that, I will be unable to photograph your son."

"Bring more lamps!" Matthew shouted at the valet in a voice which was unexpectedly harsh.

I fought back the urge to run out of the room and onto the street; the air was a poisonous fume.

Thankfully after only a few seconds the valet appeared with two more lamps. He was reluctant to bring them to me.

"Take them to him then you miserable wretch!" Matthew ordered him again.

The valet walked quickly towards me and placed the lamps on the mantelpiece.

Immediately the horror of what lay before me was revealed in a ghostly glow. There was a body, as I had expected, but what lay above the collar and tie had long ceased to be a face.

My eyes grew wide in shock and I gasped for the foul air around me. There was nothing but tendons and sinew stretched over bone and muscle. Bulging eyes stared back at me with a lifeless gaze. "What is this?" I uttered.

"Why sir, it is my son, Jonathan." Matthew spoke gently again. "Jonathan Lovett."

The name Lovett was familiar to me, as I suspect it was to all of London, if not the world. He had slain a great many men, ripping their faces to make macabre masks for his own amusement. Now, here I was, about to take a photograph of his decomposed body. What ill deeds had I done to deserve this?

I could not take my eyes from the atrocity which lay before me; I was hypnotised by the rotting corpse.

"Sir, I do not think I can take this photograph; he is too far gone." A cloud of flies gathered over the festering remains of Jonathan Lovett's face. They had clearly been disturbed from another part of his rotting body.

I heard footsteps on the oak floor beside me, yet still I could not look away. "No, you have quite misunderstood my request. I must apologise for the misunderstanding." I noticed his voice was softer that it had been when ordering the valet. With relief I looked away and gazed upon Matthew Lovett. My relief was short lived.

Matthew Lovett's face had been skeletal and unpleasant, but that was nothing as to what it had become.

"My contacts at Scotland Yard assure me this was the mask my son was wearing when he was arrested." With the shrunken skin of a dozen men stretched over his face Matthew Lovett laughed.

"And now, you shall photograph me with the face of my son; the last of the Lovett men together on an everlasting image."

A New Costume

First and foremost, I am an entertainer. Secondly, I am a killer. It may surprise you but I believe the two can be partners; uncomfortable perhaps, but with a little creativity, it can be achieved with a certain elegance. Unfortunately it means I carry no reputation as an artiste and must, inevitably, perform only in the smaller halls and theatres of this land. Whilst this somewhat demeans my soul, the anonymity it provides is a means of satisfying both my desires; to entertain and to murder.

I am fortunate enough to have been blessed with the spirit of a performer and provided with the skills to accompany that gift. It has seen me perform many roles in many genres and helped me kill many men.

As a young man I had never had much interest in the theatre but one day I passed a poster which caught my eye. It showed a man of Moorish appearance carrying a giant curved sword. There were other characters on the crude poster but he alone caught my eye; Othello it said beneath his sword. The theatre was nothing more than a ramshackle lodge and being a man of low means I took a seat in the gods. It was the first show I had seen and it was life changing. The theatre and the cast were the most beautiful things I had ever seen. I made a vow to myself that this is where I would spend my life.

I felt no connection with the man Othello or the actor himself and found myself increasingly drawn to the character Iago. His duplicity and seething madness were what attracted me so; the devious natures of his intentions were both frightening and brilliant.

The bawdy crowd booed and shouted abuse whenever he appeared and I found myself hating them all. I cheered for him and championed his cause at every opportunity, although I was alone in this. It was after my last call in his support that a fist split my lip and sprayed blood down my shirt.

"Shut up you ignorant fool. We have come to shout at the villain, not listen to your rubbish." The oaf pushed me off my seat and stole my shoes. His reeking breath smelled of gin and grease.

"Give me my shoes!" I yelled and fought to get them back but he threw them down into the stalls, where they melted away. His friends laughed until they could barely breathe and the oaf yelled at me as I hobbled away. "That'll teach you to ruin my night!"

I waited for a long time outside that theatre; in the cold drizzle of a dreary night, and when at last he left, I followed him. The brute and his drunken colleagues staggered their way through the gas lit streets; until one by one, his friends left and he was alone. I gave as little thought to what I did next as I would to picking his pocket.

He never even heard me step out from the shadows, and as I followed close behind, the stench of gin followed him like a putrid vapour. I felt hatred for that man or for what he had done to me in the theatre. The first blow split his head in a crazed line from top to bottom, and as I raised the rock to hit him again, I spied greyness beneath. It was a strange sight, for beneath the skin, I expected only blood and not this disappointing stain. He sank to his knees and uttered a guttural sound but I brought it down again, hard against his broken skull. I dropped the rock quickly and removed his battered old shoes. "And that sir, will teach you." Thus began my love for the stage and for taking a life.

I could have done the same to Mr Jonathan Lovett after what he had done to my sister. I could have split his skull like so many others but where is the skill in that? Where is the entertainment? And above all, where is the performance?

———

I watched as they took the final two generations of Lovett men away from their mansion in Belgravia. Feet first through the door they came, wrapped in white linen as pure as the snow. Yet, even from across the street, in the warmth of the cab, I could smell their decay.

"Sister? Where is my costume?" Susanna sat beside me and as always had her part to play.

"Right here my brother. Here, let me adjust the collar."

The driver, paid handsomely, drove at a deathly speed away from the house. I knew time was short before the next act began. Before long, he pulled up at the gates and I banged my cane on the roof. "We shall walk from here I think." I took my sister's arm and we walked through the grounds, just where we had walked last night. This morning, high in the yew, a dove called to its mate, where last night the owl had screeched to its prey.

"I really think this costume suits you well brother. I think this may be your finest performance yet."

"Do you think so dear? It feels a little sticky still."

"After the show, we shall wash the blood off or even better, purchase a new one."

We took our place beside the graves and waited in silence. After all this time, and after all those performances, I am a little ashamed to say I still suffer with stage fright. The mound of fresh earth beside the freshly dug graves writhed with a mass of excited worms as the procession advanced.

The pallbearers lowered the coffins beside their final destinations and stood back. I was surprised at the attendance for barely a handful of mourners had come.
Two coffins placed side by side; father and son together for eternity.

I coughed to clear my throat for the first line, and looked to the audience.

"Let us commend Matthew and Jonathan Lovett to the mercy of God. We commit their bodies to the ground; earth to earth, ashes to ashes, dust to dust; in the sure and certain hope of the Resurrection to eternal life."
The coffins were lowered into the earth.

'I wonder what entertainment I can conjure in my new role as a man of god? The possibilities, at least at the moment, seem endless.'

The End

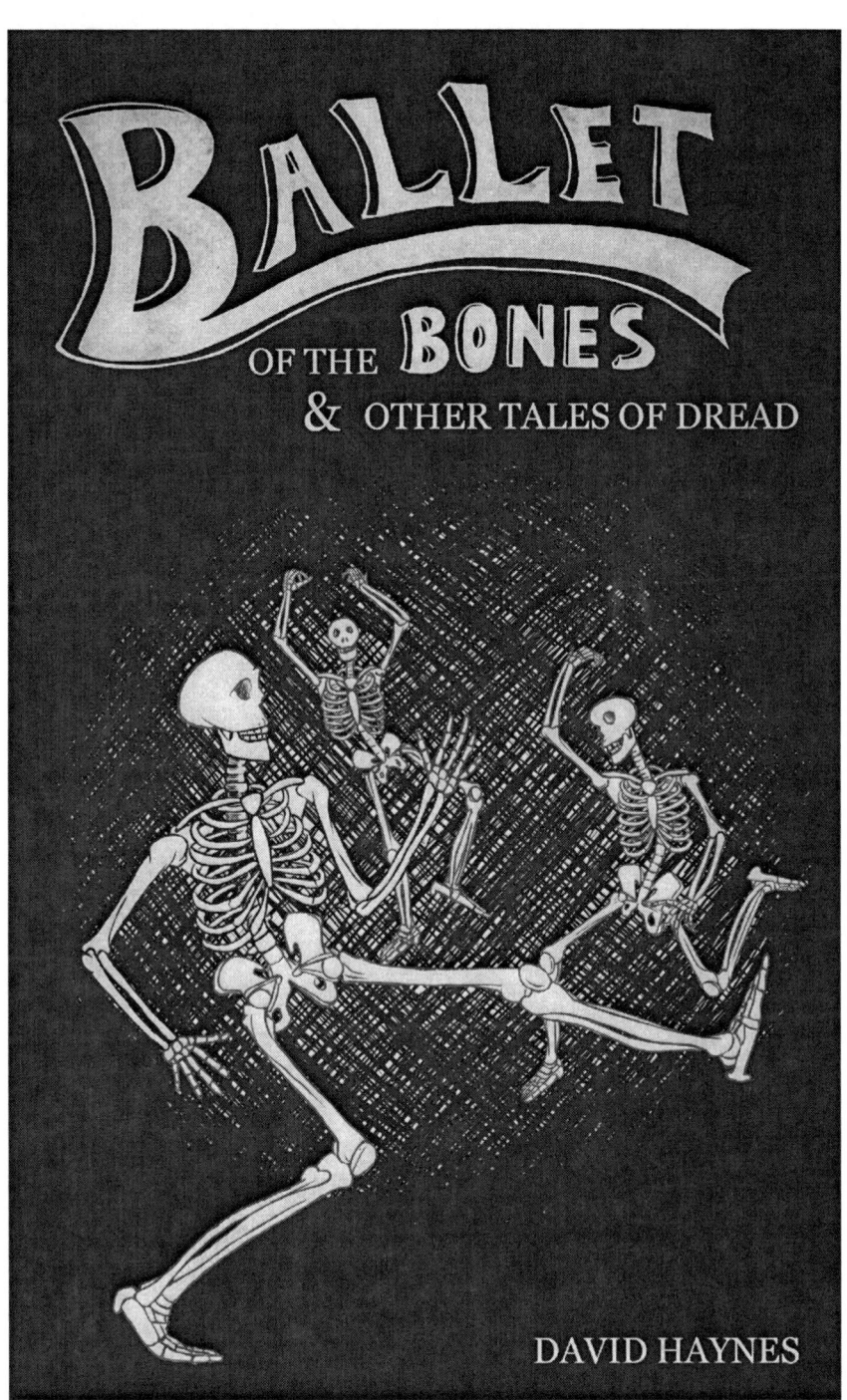

BALLET
OF THE BONES
& OTHER TALES OF DREAD

DAVID HAYNES

Ballet of the Bones

Contents

Ballet of the Bones

"This, sir is the infamous Jonathan Lovett; the murderer of a hundred men. Watch how he takes a blade to his victim's face and slices off their skin." The candles gave an eerie lustre to Lovett's malevolent sneer. I watched the crude mechanical waxwork slowly lift its arm and stop.

"Sir, I believe Lovett killed a mere ten men. No more." The gentleman said blandly and looked at his pocket watch.

The waxwork had stalled again. "Quite sir, but there may have been more. We shall never know. Not now he is sleeping with the devil." Lovett appeared to be stuck in a peculiar and unnatural jig.

The gentleman, my only customer this last week, emitted a long, drawn out sigh. In a pathetic, futile gesture Lovett's arm finally fell into place and sliced a lump of wax from the supine model.

"May I show you the Egyptian tomb display sir? They were a ghastly lot…" He had already walked away without speaking further.

The final stroke of Jonathan Lovett's knife had fallen like an auctioneer's gavel on the last lot of my haemorrhaging enterprise.

R.J. Chesterton and The Gallery of Wax had been on Drury Lane for the last fifty years. My father, before me, had created the spectacle, and with his death, I found it my responsibility to continue his work. My brother, a gifted engineer, had pioneered the use of mechanical devices in our creations. Yet, unlike me, he had little interest in either the gallery or his family and had long since forgotten my plight.

Our creations were regarded as being the most lifelike of all the wax museums in the city. Perhaps, I might venture, in the world. My most popular display; 'The Mask of The Macabre,' was at one time thought to be so terrifying a spectacle that ladies were forbidden to enter. The image of the infamous murderer, Jonathan Lovett, flaying his victims alive was without doubt our most gruesome and hideous display. It was our finest, and unfortunately, last piece of work.

"Why gaze upon a wax-work monster when the real monsters walk the streets?" These are the words I heard from my customers, not once, but on a number of occasions. They were perfectly correct of course. There were many strange, new oddities on display in the city.

A new taste for viewing poor unfortunate creatures, inflicted with diabolical deformities, had taken the public. They were said to be of such hideous proportion that the very thought was entirely unpalatable to me. It was further distasteful that this penchant was the reason behind my impending financial ruin.

In my wanderings through the East End, I noted how every other shop seemed to advertise some depraved or hideous creature for men to gaze upon. How my attention was in the first place drawn to one particular building, I cannot recall, but drawn it was.

Painted upon the window were the words; 'Fairbrother and son present: Valeria – The Fat Girl.' Was this what passed for entertainment on the once discerning palate of our society? To stand and gawp upon an oddity such as this could not surely be all there was to an evening of entertainment?

"Come to see the fat girl, sir? Never has there been such a spectacle as our Valeria." The boy, barely out of puberty, stood in the doorway shouting to all who paused long enough to hear him. I felt a compulsion finally to see what made the public clamour so greatly.

I paid the boy a penny and went into a parlour such as you would find in any house belonging to a working man. Illuminated under a cluster of candles was a lady, dressed only in her undergarments and stretched across a crimson chaise. She looked utterly bored, and if I had not known better from her dismissive sigh, I might have thought her dead. Several of the men present laughed and pointed at her before making bawdy comments regarding her attire. To my surprise she remained utterly impassive to their derision. She was undoubtedly a large lady, but given that the chaise was clearly an item manufactured for an infant, her proportions were freakishly contrived. I looked about the room and counted ten gentlemen gawking at her. That was more customers than I had attracted all this last month. With a burgeoning anger I left the parlour and continued my way through the howling wilderness the streets had become.

I entered three more shops that afternoon, for shops are all they were. Wedged between the merchants and butchers they presented a sickening façade of temptation where every one of them had a creature to flaunt. I do not know whether it was a twisted desire for fame, or whether it was for another miserable purpose but they displayed themselves with abandon.

I could not fathom why they would interest anyone so much though, for they were not the hideous monsters I had believed them to be. Yet fascinate and appal they so clearly did. It cost me a penny to ogle a fat or bearded lady and a man so covered with tattoos that none of his flesh was visible.

It was less hideous than maddening but it was a street filled with riches. As I walked through the throng with the nasal chatter of Punch ringing in my ears, I began to ponder. If I could find someone truly monstrous, truly spectacular then with my skills, knowledge and gallery I could create such a success. Was I prepared to take that abominable step into the dismal abyss of exploitation? My soul said, 'No, forever, no,' but my pride travelled swiftly along the dark and furious channels of my mind. 'Yes,' it cried. 'Yes you must. Bring R.J. Chesterton back to the top.'

Where does one find a monster though? As that clever customer remarked, the real monsters walk freely along the street. They emerge from the shadows with their blades primed and ready for a slice of flesh. That is where the real monsters live.

It was with a gamble and no small expense that I placed an advertisement in the respected periodical – The Zodiac, requesting the services of these so called 'freaks of nature.' My establishment, unlike the simple parlours and shop fronts of the East End, was built as a venue of entertainment. This advantage would allow me to accommodate eleven of these individuals, each in a gallery of their own. Thus, if the gentlemen of London were willing to part with a penny to see a single fat lady, then I felt sure they would pay three pennies to see my troupe of aberrations.

After two days of interviewing the oddities who presented themselves to my establishment I began to become somewhat immune to their appearance. Some were tricksters or fraudsters, others nothing more than a trifle unusual. Then there were the desperate creatures, for whom displaying themselves as nothing more than circus animals, was a better fate than the alternative which awaited them on the street.

As the afternoon passed into the evening, the disgust which I felt growing in my soul had manifested itself as dreadful headache. It was not loathing for them that I felt; it was for my own humanity. I could not employ these people. I could not see them displayed like beasts in this place. The Gallery of Wax had seen such elegance and flair in the past; grandiose performances at my father's hands. I would not allow it to become a crucible of malaise for my wretched heart; not now and not ever.

I lit the oil lamp in my office and hung my head. Would my father have acted any differently? Would he have had the stomach to do what I could not? I would never know the answers to these questions and I was thankful for that; I was ashamed enough already.

Thump thump thump.

Someone, undoubtedly another so-called monster, was banging on the door. I had neither the heart nor the stomach to listen to another fabricated tale of the riches their employ would surely bring. I took up the lamp and walked quickly past the shadowy forms of Lovett and his victims, through the hangman's scene and out into the narrow foyer.

"The building is closed. The auditions have finished." I shouted through the doors at the unseen guest.

"Sir, I have not come to audition, but to make you an offer." The voice of a well-spoken gentleman replied.

Was this how it happened? The carrion eaters were circling my flesh before last the breath was taken?

"I have not yet appointed an agent; you may address all enquiries through him when the position is filled. Good evening, sir."

"I have not come to make a purchase. I have come to put the name of R.J. Chesterton back where it belongs."

I opened the door a crack to see who this individual was. His appearance ,was as I had expected from his enunciation, immaculate. He touched the rim his top hat and smiled.

"William Fettiplace at your service, sir." His attire was better suited to a royal box at the theatre than my establishment.

"I am pleased to make your acquaintance, Mr Fettiplace. What can I do for you this evening?"

"Mr Chesterton, as warm as my cloak is, I wonder if I might step inside to discuss the matter further? There is a biting chill to the air this evening."

Fettiplace was clearly no ruffian come to bash my brains in for a penny, and his offer was certainly intriguing.

I opened the door and stepped aside. "Please, come in. I have an office where we can speak freely."

Fettiplace stepped inside and removed his hat. A cloud of silver hair billowed out from beneath. "I remember coming here in my youth." He smiled again. "Amongst other places of course; shall we?"

I led him along the corridor, past the small stages where the exhibits were kept. Each one was presented as if it were a theatre on its own, complete with curtains and set. He was particularly interested in the Jonathan Lovett display. "Ah yes, the infamous Jonathan Lovett. Now there was a creature, make no mistake. May I?" He took the lamp from my grasp and held it beneath Lovett's face. "It is a particularly good likeness Mr Chesterton, particularly good. That was before he was caught and mutilated himself, of course."

"You met him, sir?"

___

54

Fettiplace handed the lamp back. "I never had the pleasure. I merely recognised him from the sketches in The Times."

"I'm not sure if the most appropriate description of a meeting with him would be 'a pleasure.' He remained silent and stared at the silhouette of the murderer for a second or two.

"He was a fascinating character, nonetheless." He appeared transfixed by the model.

"My office is this way." I started walking off down the corridor leaving him in the dark.

"I should like to speak here, if we may?"

"I don't mind where we speak." I walked back to where Fettiplace had remained.

"I read, with interest, the advertisement you placed in The Zodiac, Mr Chesterton." A pained look appeared on his otherwise unperturbed countenance. "I frequently read the journal in my capacity as a man of entertainment. I must say it troubled me somewhat that an establishment such as this should encourage the growth in that monstrous industry." He waved his hand at the darkened exhibits. "This has theatre. This has such majesty as you would see on the finest stages in London. Why would one want simply to watch a bearded woman display herself? Or watch a midget stand on a chair? There is no showmanship to it sir, none at all. You, on the contrary, have a story to tell. Beneath all of these models is a story. Each one is a unique tale of despair or of violence, of the human spirit gone awry; and of course in dear old Lovett's case, murder."

His fervour for my tired exhibition was invigorating and infectious. "I believe so too Mr Fettiplace but alas the public do not. They want to be appalled and to scoff at those poor creatures. I cannot compete and thus I felt compelled to advertise. It is something I now bitterly regret."

Fettiplace placed his hand on my shoulder. "Chesterton, worry no more. We shall do more than compete, we shall surpass them. Leave that with me."

Together, over brandy, we discussed the matter at length. Our arrangement was simple. Fettiplace would provide the exhibits and the elaborate flourishes about which he was clearly excited. He assured me the theatricality of a show was his speciality. I was simply to provide the premises.

The profits, if there were any, would simply be divided into two equal portions; and if the venture were unsuccessful then he would leave within the week. Upon my questions about the nature of the show, his reply was as simple as our arrangement.

"No man, nor woman shall be displayed within these walls, I assure you of that."

I was at the point where I had nothing left to lose. In a week, what could possibly happen to worsen my fortune? It seemed an easy decision. Why then, for all Fettiplace's charm, did I feel a nagging sense of disquiet slowly creep into my mind?

In the days that followed, Fettiplace and his associates filled my establishment with boxes, crates and vessels of a variety of sizes. I was forbidden to look inside. "Fettiplace, I do not know what you have planned but your reluctance to reveal your show concerns me."

"Chesterton, you are a foolish and cautious man. They are my masterpieces and that is all. They have been specifically designed to thrill and disturb. London has never have seen the likes of these before, I can assure you of that! Now, go home and light a pipe, when you return their true brilliance will be on display."

I left him there and walked briskly through the noisy street, past the excited masses tumbling their way out from the theatres and onto The Strand. Most of all I wanted to speak with my father, to take his counsel on what I should do. For all his bluster, Fettiplace's plans had left me weary and even more convinced that the future of my enterprise was surely doom laden. My mood was one of despair.

My father had been a generous and caring man with a rare talent and that talent was to amuse and distract people from the grime of their everyday life. With an artist's touch he gave life to his models of wax like he was the creator himself. He had also been a pious man, and even in the forlorn shadow of my mother's coffin, he clung to his religion with the tips of his aching fingers.

It was only natural to him that when his gift yielded riches, some of those treasures should be shared among those less fortunate that himself. It was with an unending sense of disappointment that I always felt ill equipped to continue with any of his work, altruistic or otherwise.

Many times during the six months since his passing I had come to St. Mary Le Strand church to seek his guidance. The church was a serene and proud building, set quietly amongst the raucous cacophony of The Strand. The black hooded cabs and carriages swirled around its base like a swarm of carrion flies to a corpse. Yet, for all its resolute composure, it was losing ground to a changing city.

The inexorable passage of man beneath the watchful gaze of its baroque tower, pounded away at its diminishing boundaries. My father's burial had been the last in the cemetery, his body at peace beside my mother. Both of them had been buried with the key to his dream around their decaying necks; the key to The Gallery of Wax. Their interment had only been permitted because of his eternal bequest of a hundred pounds a year; an obligation I would be unable to fulfil.

The London Necropolis Company had already established Brookwood cemetery, some distance from the city. The authorities hoped that all the graves would be emptied and their rotting contents reinterred in Brookwood. How this sickening undertaking would be achieved was well left to those with a stronger stomach than I. Yet, it had already begun, at least for those unfortunate souls with families unable to petition their bodies to remain.

Alone, beneath the shadow of a giant old yew, I found my father's grave and knelt beside him. The clatter of hooves on the cobbles and the cries of demented drivers was nothing more than a distant hum to me now.

"Father, I have failed." I hung my head in shame, for even in death his presence was strong. "I have made a ruin of the gallery and of your name." I raised my head and glanced away. In my ignominy I felt unable to look upon his headstone any longer. Under the faint light of a distant lamp, I could see the removal work had begun in earnest and mounds of fresh earth littered the graveyard. How many had gone already? I held my face in my hands. I knew at that moment my parents would be taken to Brookwood along with the others and there was nothing I could do to prevent it. Perhaps, I wondered, it would be a better fate for all if I went with them.

I arrived at my premises early the next morning for I had barely slept a minute that night. My nightmares were filled with ghastly images of death and decay where men slaughtered each other for fun.

When I arrived I found Fettiplace and his ungodly crew already hard at work. "Ah, here he is, Chesterton himself. You look a little under the weather, sir; here have this." He thrust a silver flask into my hand and I took a sip of the brandy within.

"Now, Chesterton, come and see what marvels I have created." He took me by the shoulder and ushered me inside. I could see the shadow of the morning's growth on his chin.

"Have you been here all night?"

His enthusiasm was without bounds and only matched by his energy. "Of course I have. We all have." He waved at the filthy vagabonds marching in and out of my establishment as if it were their own. "There is no time to waste Chesterton. I intend to open the show today. How do you feel about this? He gave such a flourish to his hands that it was almost a performance in itself. "R.J. Chesterton presents - Ballet of the Bones."

"It certainly sounds enticing, if not disturbing. It seems a little unfair since you have been the instigator of its conception. Can we not add the name Fettiplace to the title somewhere?"

"Most certainly not; I want you to take the credit for this. Besides how will I alter this at such short notice?"

He unrolled a sheet of paper and held it out before me. It was a beautiful poster, the likes of which I had seldom seen before, except on the frontage of the Theatre Royal. In simple yet elaborate lines the artist had sketched two skeletons clinging together like macabre lovers. The bones of another formed the letters 'Ballet of the Bones' and all around the edge were skulls, grinning and laughing silently at the morbid dancers.

I was aghast. "It is quite astonishing."

"You like it then Chesterton?" Fettiplace began laughing and clutching his belly.

"It belongs somewhere far greater than here. I cannot afford the expense."

"Nonsense, my sister is a very talented artist. They are being glued to every lamp-post and wall between here and Parliament, as we speak. Tonight we open!"

"Will it all be ready?" There was so much movement that I could barely fathom who was doing what. A harmonium was being dragged carelessly inside by a group of men who seemed unconcerned by its size or weight. "Of course we'll be ready. R.J. Chesterton will be back where it belongs." Fettiplace pushed past the men and led me, like a child, inside.

From the beguilingly sinister poster I had an idea what Fettiplace was planning but his first display left me cold.

"The crucifixion," he pronounced as we entered the corridor. Before my eyes a carpenter was constructing a crude wooden cross. At his feet lay two skeletons, one with a crown of thorns.

"You cannot display this, it is blasphemy!" I shouted.

"You are being too sensitive. This is recreated in every church in the world."

I turned to see his uncouth smile. "But we are not a church!"

"But what is a church, if not a theatre to show the greatest story ever told?" Fettiplace stepped over the crimson cord which marked the threshold of the display. "Your mechanical devices are crude but I have a man skilled in the adjustment necessary to make this display a true performance." He took hold of the pile of bones which had set whole again. "This one will hold the Spear of Destiny and drive it into the ribs of Christ, in perpetuity."

"This is monstrous. I will not allow it." I turned my back on the hideous display.

"And yet you do nothing to stop it. You have given up hope, you have lost everything and yet you cling to some notion of nobility like a fool. What do you think of the men who gawp at the aberrations God created? The deformed monsters displayed in the parlours up and down every street in this twisted city? Are they not blasphemous? Do they not mock His creations?" Fettiplace's tone was harsh and scolding.

"I cannot..." I gasped.

I felt a hand on my shoulder. "You know this is nothing more than theatre and you know they will clamour for it." His tone was as soft and gentle as a father reading to a child.

"Three pennies a piece; think of the wealth and consider your father."

———

I turned on him. "What do you know of my father? He would roll in his grave to see something such as this in his beloved creation."

"Your father will roll in his grave if you destroy his creation Chesterton. Now come and see the other displays. I shall endeavour to change your mind."

One by one, Fettiplace showed me his ghastly conceptions, all as abhorrent as the first.

'Three pennies a piece.'

He led me through a never ending skeletal ballet of the most horrific and entirely biblical proportions. On the first stage the show was the martyrdom of Saint Bartholomew. Were it not for the flap of his flayed skin being swung like a toy by another skeleton, it would have been a sedentary display. On the next stage I was treated to a display of Simon the Zealot being sawn in half whilst he was crucified.

"Enough, Fettiplace; I cannot bear to see a single further atrocity. We will be lucky to escape with our lives after this."

Fettiplace laughed; a cold and unpleasant sound. "We're not in biblical times any longer. Religion holds a great deal less influence than it did back then."

"Sacrilege is eternal. I shall remain in my office until the very last person has left."

"As you wish, but you will be missing a wonderful show. Why, you haven't seen the beheading of Paul yet."

I held up my hand and walked slowly to the office; I would hear no more of this. The only solace I sought now was in the pungent warmth of a bottle of brandy.

———

The excited chatter of an expectant audience was something The Gallery of Wax had not heard for a very long time. It was with a degree of exhilaration that, as my watch struck seven, I heard Fettiplace's cheerful voice declare. "Ladies and gentlemen, step inside and witness a show of such wickedness you will fear for your very souls."

I could hear the hum of voices beyond my office, and more importantly, I could hear the pleasant ring of coin against coin.

Almost immediately there was a scream from the corridor. 'So it begins.' I thought. 'They will be upon me in a matter of seconds and I will be the one beheaded, not Paul.' I needn't have worried though for in the next second the scream turned to laughter and my anxiety quietened. Could I be so out of touch with society? Was blasphemy now the entertainment of the masses? The harmonium played a familiar Bach fugue to lament the demise of our Skeleton Lord, but it was accompanied by the repulsive laughter of his eternally lost followers. I hung my head in shame. 'Three pennies a piece,' it might as well have been thirty silver coins for the loathing I felt.

When at last I felt able to venture from the shadow of my office, I found Fettiplace stepping in a spritely manner among the substantial gathering. None of the oil lamps had been lit; instead hundreds of candles threw a ghostly light around the walls. He was dressed as a morbid funeral mute and holding a six foot staff covered in a delicate black crape in one hand. In the other he held a small candelabrum.

It was evident the solemnity of his attire in no way reflected his mood. I could see the amber caresses of the flames light one half of his cheerful face, "At last, Chesterton appears from his dreary closet!" He clapped me on the shoulder. The dismal sound of the harmonium echoed throughout the building. Not even when my father was alive had so many people been inside at one time.

"I don't understand how we have evaded the noose." I uttered and looked from one face to another. They gathered round each of the stages and gazed upon the grisly downfall of one apostle after another. A shocking concoction of repugnance, horror but above all, glee was clearly etched upon their faces. I began to wonder if they were not some aged wax creation my father had made.

Fettiplace held a purse before my nose and shook it. The sound of copper pennies dancing against each other brought me back to my senses.

"My, you are a grim fellow. Would three hundred pennies lighten your mood?" He jangled the purse enticingly again. I looked at the prize and then back at the man holding it. Half of that amount was more than I had taken in the last year.

"Here, hold it." He placed the velvet bag into my waiting hand and I felt the pleasurable weight of its value. Against my strongest desire, a thin smile toyed with my lips.

"There you go; a smile from the man at last." Fettiplace laughed again and walked off towards a group of gentlemen gathered around the crucifixion.

As the clock struck midnight more than one hundred and fifty visitors had come through the doors at Fettiplace's show. As I left, still more arrived, smelling of the gin houses from whence they came.

———

My spirits had lifted, of that there was no doubt, but I wanted to be gone from the place. I needed to be away from Fettiplace, his diseased sense of humour and those damned macabre disciples.

In my bed I waited for unconsciousness to bring the deathly shadows that my haunted dreams had become. The Gallery of Wax was saved, due entirely to Fettiplace, but at what price to my soul? There had been dark, dark days after my mother had died when my father could barely rise from his bed; when he wept like a child and asked of his Lord, 'Why have you taken her Lord, what have I done?' Yet, even in those days, consorting with the devil had never been considered. It would break my father's heart to see the gallery collapse; but far worse, it would destroy his soul to observe it tonight. I had settled my mind; Fettiplace and his disgraceful aberrations would be gone in the morning. His departure would signal the death knell for the gallery but remove a great weight from my drained soul.

My dreams came and went throughout the night. Some were fleeting whilst others lingered, leaving a poisonous scar. My sleep had become a place where a tuneless piano played melancholy chords and the shadows danced a dismal waltz.

In the dreary gloom of my room I was cheered to see the first of the morning light. It brought an end to my tormented night. I dressed quickly, for I had one visit to make before I returned to the gallery and to Fettiplace.

I walked the short distance to St Mary Le Strand at pace. I would give no opportunity for doubt to creep once more into my tired mind. I would tell my father what I had done and how completely I had failed and that was all I could do.

The Strand was not yet the raucous cacophony of hoof and bellow which it soon would be and I was thankful. It allowed me to walk directly into the churchyard without reason to pause. On either side of the path, more graves had been taken in the night; removed by The London Necropolis Company and taken away. There, probably in the company of a murderer or other profane denizen of the city, they would rest for eternity.

I walked quickly on. None of them could fight their cause to remain and had been taken I was sure, against their will. It was maddening. With a feeling of anger I arrived at the giant old yew, and to my father's grave. For a moment I believed I was in the wrong spot, confused in my weary condition; but it was not the case. Where once had lain my father's bones, was now nothing more than a mound of fresh earth. I collapsed to my knees and pushed my hands into the dirt. It was done, I was too late.

I do not recall the exact detail of my journey back to the gallery, for I was a lost man. I could not see past the grim solitude which my life had become. Was this all I had now? Nothing more than a blasphemous ballet with a lunatic lead?

I reached the gallery and found it calm. There was no trace of what had passed the night before and, most importantly, no sign of Fettiplace. I unlocked the door and stepped inside. It was cool and dark, as it always was first thing in the morning. I had grown used to the bustle and chatter of his men and their absence was all the more noticeable in the gloom.

"Hello?" I called out. No reply was given. I took up the gas lamp and began the walk to my office. I did not want to look away from the lamp, nor did I wish to see the appalling spectacle of the crucifixion or the other abominations. Inevitably, like so many others, I was drawn into the miserable world he had created.

It was, firstly, with a sense of relief I noticed the first stage was empty. The scene of Christ's downfall had been taken away. 'Had London finally come to its lost senses?' I dismissed the thought. Had that been the case, the gallery would have been subjected to wrath, the like of which was last witnessed in Sodom and Gomorrah.

By the time I reached the final gallery it was clear that Fettiplace had taken his grisly enterprise with him. I was thankful for this, for it would negate the need for any disagreeable confrontations with the man. For all his charm, there was something disturbing in his cold eyes; something which told me he was a man well versed in conflict.

The last gallery remained covered by its scarlet curtain. It looked strangely out of place, as if Fettiplace had neglected it in his haste to leave.

I drew back the curtain and was confronted by the awful truth of his show. The last of the apostles was waiting just for me. Several pieces of wood had been crudely nailed together to form a makeshift tree. Hung by the neck from this tree was a rotting skeleton. The bones were raised then lowered by some clever mechanical device and here and there ragged threads of a morning suit still clung to the fragile frame in helpless decay. Here and there, I could see the last fetid pieces of flesh falling away from the bone; and above the skeleton it read – 'The Death of Judas Iscariot.'

I stepped over the threshold and into the terrible display. Why had he left only this? Was it another one of his humourless jokes? In the gloom I stepped upon something and almost lost my footing. I knew, without looking, exactly what it was; Fettiplace's purse of ill-gotten gains. I kicked it away for I wanted no part of that money or where it had come from. It struck the base of the arboreal gallows sending the corpse into a frantic and ghoulish jig. As the skeleton danced, the last of the threads of the suit dropped silently to the floor and revealed a golden key around its neck. My father's key. My father's bones.

The Bone House

My elevation from an existence destined to wallow in the festering immorality of a perishing city was, some say, a matter of good fortune. I disagree with this notion, preferring to regard it as an act of a cruel, pitiless and nihilistic sovereign.

The court of King Cholera was not filled with golden goblets of spiced wine, or of sweet scented lilies. No, instead it was filled with the putrefying flesh of a thousand diseased souls. It was place where even Saint Peter feared to tread. Yet, for the fortunate ones who returned, the loathsome monarch bestowed upon them something more important than just the restoration of their health. He made them see what had gone before and vow not to return.

My family grovelled at the King's rotten feet for many days before he finally granted them passage. My father, mother and two sisters, were taken and thrust deep into the silent abyss where they waited in shadow for my demise. For reasons I do not pretend to comprehend I was allowed to walk free of the King's embrace and resume my worthless life.

I scavenged in the gutters and filth; eating any decayed scraps of food I could find and wishing I had been taken too. I slept in the street under the watchful stare of the dossers who thought me better off in a workhouse. Or, I rested on the embankment, where I was routinely beaten by those even less worthy of life than I. I was utterly destitute and asked of my God why I had been kept alive, if only to perish in such a tormented and execrable way.

It was with little comfort that I took to sleeping within the grey and silent confines of St Mary Le Strand graveyard. Many regard graveyards as desolate places filled with the stench of death, but not I. To me, it was a place of safety and of peace. My parents and sisters had been thrown into a giant pit, a pit they called a grave. Were it not for the hurried incoherent muttering of the clergymen, they would have been treated no better than animal carcasses.

Each week the pit was re-opened and a fresh collection of cadavers was thrown carelessly atop the current residents. It may seem a grim and forlorn place to spend the night and indeed it was; sleeping amongst the stinking miasma of a hundred rotting corpses. Though, each night, as I placed my weary head on the earth, I felt the warmth of my dead family seep through the worm-ridden soil. Their distant heartbeats crept through the soil and decaying flesh and beat in terrible unison with mine. How could this be of comfort? Comfort was not all I sought; I slept with the dead and dreamt their poison would make me one of them.

It was after a cold and desperate night on the grave that I was woken by the sharp jab in the ribs.

"Hook it, you miserable rogue!"

I looked up and saw the toothless snarl of the perpetrator.

"I've got work to do and I don't need some vagabond getting in the way." He raised a staff and brought it down on my legs.

I covered my head. "Please, sir. No more. I was only trying to take some kip."

"Well take it somewhere else." He kicked me in the stomach with his filthy boot.

I rose to my feet and felt the cold ache of a night without shelter writhe through my bones. The morning was bitter and as drab as my beaten spirit. I had nowhere else to go and no hope for relief from my anguish. It was with a jaded interest that I watched the man set to work.

With a great sigh he plunged a rod into the earth beside the communal pit. His efforts met with a small amount of resistance, but he continued and pushed deeper into the earth until the rod was almost sunk entirely. Immediately a vile stench pervaded the air and caused me to retch. The man glanced with little concern at my empty heave and continued with his hideous toil.

When at last he was satisfied with the results of his survey, he took up his shovel. Each strike of the blade sent a fresh cloud of rancid air into my lungs; and yet he seemed entirely oblivious to it and whistled like a lark as he worked.

The ground was soft, and after the passage of only a few minutes, he dropped into the pit of his labour. He may as well have been dressed in a black cloak, carrying a scythe for his next act was one of death. Bone, after splintered bone, he pulled from the earth. Slack jawed skulls with their gossamer hair, and eye sockets packed full of mud; he cared not for their state and piled them beside the pit with his naked hands. Was he robbing the graves? I considered it quickly for I had heard of such matters in the North; yet what was the purpose? There was nothing of value, for the trinkets, if there were any, had been taken long before now.

With a grunt he pulled himself clear and kicked the bones carelessly into a sack. He heaved it onto his broad, strong back and walked away from the stench. It struck me that I should call for a constable, or maybe even take up the rod and strike him down.

Instead, in my bewildered interest I followed him across the graveyard to a small, yet sinister looking building. It had a crude and functional appearance and was in contrast to the elegant scrolls and majestic angels which adorned the tops of the headstones.

For this reason, it was hidden from view, away from the quiet beauty of the dead and their solemn visitors. He opened the door to the building with a kick from his boot allowing the weak morning light to penetrate within. I could see it was no larger than the pathetic room my family and I had shared before we fell ill. I peered from my vantage and watched him stoke a fire in the grate until it roared and hissed. As cold as I was I would not venture into that place for a second for it filled me with dread.

Without further ceremony he tipped the sack onto the fire and in a hissing cacophony the bones were ablaze. The flames whipped around the bones and sent tongues of burning rapture through the voids where once eyes had lived. A poisonous black fume was sent up through the chimney and out into grey sky. It was carried away in an instant by the cool winter wind and into the lungs of the ignorant inhabitants of the city. In a sickening final insult to those he had destroyed, he rubbed his hands, warmed them against the pyre and pushed his coffee pot into the coals.

I shrank back from the view; I could not stand to look at it further. What right had he to dispose of them in that manner?

I retched, a dry and desperate sound for I had not eaten a morsel for two days.

"I told you to get out of here." I felt the familiar boot in my ribs and fell to the floor.

72

"A bit sour for you is it?" I heard his sick cackle as he walked away.

Was this the ruthless fate awaiting my family?

"Wait, sir!" I called after him as he whistled his way back across the graveyard. "Please don't."

"We gotta make room for the new 'uns, there's always lots of new 'uns, now The King is in town."

He pushed his rod into the spot where not an hour since I lay in a fitful slumber. "Stop!" I called, yet he refused to acknowledge my presence.

"Stop!" I called again. My family were below him and I would not allow them to be disturbed by this filthy animal. I knew what I must do.

His shovel, discarded in haste to rifle through the bones with his bare hands, lay in the mud. I took it in my hands and felt the strength of its uncouth purpose flow through my arms. "Stop!" I called for the last time, and as he turned with a vile sneer, I brought it down on his head. The sickening shudder of shovel on bone rang through the handle with a jarring force and sent us both flailing into the freshly dug pit. As our bodies came together in a jumble of mud, I screamed at the agony of my fate; I roared at him because there was no other. Then, when my voice gave out, I beat his face with my fists until the blood made gloves of my hands.

I do not know if he was dead at that moment, but as I clambered out from his pit and piled earth over his face, I knew he soon would be.

"Bravo!" A voice called from beyond my view but I continued with my gory task; I had no wish to hang. "Boy?" The voice came again. It was an enquiring voice, not the brusque tone I was used to.

I piled one last shovel of earth over his face and turned to see who was calling. A well-dressed man smiled as he approached. His cloak flew out from his back like the wings of a crow and he tapped his cane on the headstones as he passed by.

"You must be the new grave digger then, boy?"

I stared at my feet for this was clearly a gentleman and I had felt the biting sting of a cane before.

"Come, let us get acquainted in the warmth of the bone house." I felt the weight of his gloved hand on my shoulder. "What a marvellously brutal performance you just produced, although it lacked the true flair of a showman." He peered into the pit and smiled. "I can see we have matters to discuss, you and I. What is your name?"

I remained silent.

"Well, allow me introduce myself first then? William Fettiplace is my name, and some say devilment is my game." His bright and cheery laugh was sufficient to tempt me to his side and into the bone house.

I felt no remorse for my actions. I felt only relief that the grave digger had failed to make my family a wisp of smoke carried away on the wind.

Nearly twenty years have passed since that day and when I recall the episode I feel only satisfaction; not in the act of murder, rather in the wheels that act set in motion.

It gave my previously wretched existence a purpose. Grave diggers are, by necessity and nature, a drunken, violent and miserable lot. I was not of this nature and so quickly established a position within the district as master of my profession. I overcame my aversion to the burning of bones, except of course, for the bones of my family, whose nameless grave, I fiercely guarded.

In the warmth of the bone house I would oft sit conversing with the sprightly crackle of a burning skull. There, I would warm my hands as their chatter was silenced forever in the heat of my pyre.

"Goodnight,Pa," or "Goodnight Ma," I would say as they were finally consumed. I fancied the larger skulls belonged to men and the smaller ones to women; the skulls belonging to infants I burned without comment. From time to time a gentleman would appear from the shadows and request my sack of bones in exchange for a few pennies. I cared not for his purpose for the pennies were welcome and the bones destined for the pyre.

In the confinement of my life within the beautiful churchyard I found the company of the dead to be, by and large, preferable to that of the living. The company of Mr Fettiplace excluded, of course.

I learned to read by tracing my fingers over the lichen-covered names on the headstones as we strolled about them. It was of no great surprise that the first words I could pen were the insipid inscriptions carved into the stone.

The long, cold nights, I would spend huddled in the bone house, basking in the heat of the eternal glare from the pyre. The flames were never extinguished, not even for a moment, for the dead came two by two on their bleak pilgrimage to my door. "Gotta make room for the new 'uns." I would say as I tipped them into the fire.

For too many years had London lived under the sordid influence of King Cholera's court and on that count, if none other, The Parliament agreed. An Act was passed and a great many opportunities arose for a man with my skills and lack of sensibility. Exhuming the dead had been my life's work, and with the education Mr Fettiplace had imparted, I was in an enviable position. I was made a clerk for the London Necropolis Company and the decisions I made were seldom questioned. None of my peers had set foot in a graveyard, save to mourn the passage of a loved one, and even then their gesture was fleeting.

It was a simple plan. Those buried within the city confines would be exhumed and moved to alternative lodgings where there was room for all. No longer would the bone house bear witness to the scream of smouldering ribs or the stench of blazing flesh. Its once proud hearth would be quietened forever.

Even though my elevation brought with it riches beyond my dreams or expectations it took me away from my beloved family. No longer could I spend the day talking with my father, my mother or sisters about this and that. No longer could I afford the luxury to sit and imagine the life of those I set ablaze in my house of bones. Now my task was simple and exact; I was to make arrangements for bones to be sent to Brookwood Cemetery.

With each grave exhumed, I clung to the hope that St Mary le Strand would be spared; that somehow the city would stop its infernal growth and my family would be left in peace. When time allowed I would walk to the square of earth where my family lay. So long had it remained untouched, protected by the steady hand of my guardianship, that here and there white snowdrops grew, caring not what lay beneath.

It was during one of these strolls through my previous life that I met my beloved Lucy. She shivered, cold and lonely in the gloom of the bone house waiting for me to come. I believe a beautiful fate guided me to her that evening, and as I wrapped my coat around her that cold night, I knew we would be together for all eternity. She has remained with me ever since that day and we have been blessed with a child, a poor sickly boy who can scarce leave his bed. It has long been a regret that my parents and sisters were never granted the time to meet Lucy and my son, William. They have much in common.

There is much silence between my wife and me now, for we both know that our wretched William is not long for this world. I am ashamed to say that I cannot abide to be in my abode for longer than is necessary; preferring to fill my mind with the complexities of my work. To think what may become of my son is too great an ordeal to suffer.

Mr Fettiplace appeared from time to time over the years, seeing something in the performance of my savage act of murder which appealed to his nature. Yet, until this last week, he asked for nothing in return.

The time had come for St Mary le Strand to cede to the passage of man. I could delay the matter no longer. The eternal miasma which clung to the church, threatened, with each passing day, to erupt and spew forth its foul reek. Overcome with grief, I wandered to their resting place and wept beside the grave. In a repeat of the morning many years before, Mr Fettiplace appeared at my side.

"Grieve for them, Thomas and grieve for them well." My simple clerk's suit was nothing to his splendid attire. Had the church bells not struck eleven in the grey morning light, I would have thought he were theatre bound.

"I wish for twelve of your bodies. Eleven from anywhere you choose," he swung his cane in a great arc, "and one from a particular spot. Can you arrange this Thomas?"

His smile was the least attractive feature of his character, for in it I spied a wicked man, a man with more than just devilment on his mind.

"Of course, sir. Which particular grave interests you?"

"A fellow by the name of Chesterton. Over there under the yew." He pointed his cane to the farthest corner of the graveyard. "I should like them delivered here." He handed me a card. "I will expect discretion, Thomas."

I did not ask his purpose in securing these bones, for what good would come from it? Besides, at that moment I was committed to my misery. Mr Fettiplace had often spoken of matters I did not understand, matters of a personal nature which were disturbing. I am not a sensitive man; as you have heard I committed the gravest of crimes, yet even to me, there were times when his manner was debauched. It was clear he was a man for whom a grudge was debt unpaid.

I instructed my troupe of grave diggers to remove the oldest corpses from the ground, and ensuring they were as complete as possible, deliver them to the address on Mr Fettiplace's card. The men worked by night and asked no questions a few extra pennies could not quieten.

I had not been present during exhumation since I had completed the task myself and the effect on me was startling and unexpected. As the men worked in silence, for I would not permit idle chatter or tuneless whistle to disturb the dead, I stood and watched amid the snowdrops of my growing disquiet. I had never felt fear before; not even when I was beaten on the embankment or when I split the grave digger's head in two, yet tonight I was afraid. I was fearful I would never again lie with my father, mother and sisters or idly pass the time of day in conversation with them, until I too passed through the veil.

I sank to my knees and grasped the soil between my fingers, caring not when the men stopped and looked at me. I would not leave my parents to rot in the pit any longer, nor would I allow them to be taken to Brookwood and lie discarded like animal carcasses. I could not permit the carrion to strip whatever flesh was left from their bones and demean them further.

"Pass me a shovel!" I demanded of the nearest ruffian. He meekly obliged, fearing the tone of my voice.

The shovel sank deep with the first push, feeling no resistance below. Again I pushed the shovel deeper, sensing the ache deep in my clerk's back. The blade slipped through the earth like a knife through softened butter until it found what had been concealed for so long.

With a furious speed I exhumed bone after miserable bone, skull after rotting skull until at last I found them, huddled together in a gruesome quartet.

"Give me a sack, any of you!" I shouted into the dark graveyard. A murmur rose from the men. "Silence!" I shouted again.

I loaded the first of the bones carefully into the sack and felt the first tears stroke the soiled flesh on my cheeks. "Hello again Pa, hello Ma. Milly and Nancy. I've come to take you home. Would you like to meet Lucy and William? You remember, my wife and boy. They would so love to meet you." I caressed the mud away from their eyes. "I'll fetch us a carriage, won't that be grand!"

I walked the short distance onto the Strand and hailed a Hansom to take me home. The tormented despair I felt in the graveyard had diminished, leaving behind an excited glee. I had yearned for the unity of my family for so long and now it was a reality. It may, I fancied, provide poor William with the spirit to leave his bed.

"Lucy?" I called. There was no reply, which was often the case in these times. "Lucy, we have guests, very important guests."

I reproached myself immediately. In my excitement I had quite forgotten it was the middle of the night. Lucy and William would be sound asleep, together in the same bed.

I lit a lamp and slung the sack over my shoulder. My suit was a ruinous mess of filth from my exertions, but I cared not. Tonight was for family, not personal pride.

As quietly as I could I pushed the bedroom door open and stepped lightly inside. The room was cold but in the dim shadow of the lamp I could see the shapes of my wife and son beneath the covers.

"Lucy? William?" I whispered.

The sack had become heavy and as I lowered it onto the bed, the bones rattled against each other with dark excitement.

The flame from the lamp flickered briefly in an unseen draught before it finally settled on my wife and son. The orange glow swirled gently on their polished skulls and amber waves broke in the cavernous pools where their eyes had been decades before. They were beautiful and they were my family.

"Lucy, William. I'd like to introduce my family." I whispered and tipped the sack onto the bed. The generations of my family danced together in a melancholy skeletal embrace. We were together again, all of us.

The Engineer

I can scarce recall a time when my mind was not filled with matters of a mechanical nature. I do not know from where this simple pleasure derived and I do not query its origin. It is a blessing and it is one from which I am able to derive a living of comfortable, if unspectacular means. Although my lack of standing and qualification has prevented me from acceptance within the spheres of industrial and engineering influence, it is not a source of chagrin. It was this lack of acceptance which drove me to inhabit a place where I would be considered a master of my craft, not merely one of the crowd.

My workshop is situated in a quiet yard, thus providing clients with the discretion a visit to my premises demands. There can be no garish shop front displaying my wares, for the instruments I produce are not to the taste of all in our society. My work is for a more discerning palate, select and creative. I do not fashion the simple toys of an infant's dreams, nor do I peddle amusements for a gentleman's parlour. No, it is the instruments of their darkest desires I craft.

I had not always been a purveyor of such articles though. My skills were initially utilised in a far more conventional manner. Having left the restrictive confines of my family I was at once employed in the repair of machinery on a commercial and industrial basis. I worked as apprentice to a tiresome man, a man whose skills were infinitely inferior to my own. His concerns lay between the legs of the East End dollymops, not in the proficiency of his work. This resulted in a short apprenticeship for my teacher quickly realised the breadth of my skill and released me from obligation.

My father, although disappointed with my decision not to join him and my brother in their endeavours, bequeathed me, on his death, a not inconsiderable amount of wealth. This was to the utter displeasure of my brother, who felt it my duty to line his pockets, since he was the elder. I refused, citing that father had left the money to me, and to me alone, to do with it as I saw fit. This left Richard with only a failing business, and in his anger he vowed never to see me again.

Sadness and regret filled my life for many a month and the attempts I made to reconcile were treated with disdain and animosity. It was true, I could have given Matthew the money, or at least a part, yet I would not release it. Within that purse were not merely the paper notes of our father's fortune but the chance to become something more than he had been, or my brother would ever become. It was my life, my money and I would use it as I saw fit, not he.

I purchased my workshop in a quiet yard, not because of the need for discretion; that was not a consideration then. It was financial necessity that governed my choice. I purchased a press, tools and equipment to allow me to make a business and took my first commission within a week. Repairing sewing machines was never a line of work I envisaged taking, but the mundane nature of it permitted my mind the space to wander and conjure.

Many proud and noble men had been mutilated in the horrors of the Crimea. The once sharp wit of their agile minds was now filled with the tormented screams of their fallen comrades. The lithe strength of their young limbs lay shattered and buried in the blood soaked mud of Balaklava.

It was such a man who, by chance, appeared at my workshop door.

"May I be of service, sir?" I asked. This was clearly a gentleman of distinction who held himself with pride, as men of his class always do.

"You are an engineer?" He enquired, the vapour of his warm breath made steam in the cold air.

"Will you step inside? My hearth is warm."

The gentleman glanced over his shoulder into the quiet yard before stepping over the threshold. He wore a countenance of such wretchedness that I thought him liable to weep at any moment. The pallor of his grey and waxy skin matched his mood perfectly.   I ushered him to the warmth of the grate. "Would you care for brandy? I cannot vouch for the quality but the warming properties are without reproach."

With some effort and discomfort he raised his gloved hand. "I do not take alcohol." He looked about the workshop. "I am not sure you will be able to help me."

I was eager not to lose his custom. "Let us discuss your needs and if I am unable to aid you then you have lost nothing, save for a few moments of your time."

He sighed deeply. "Very well. I am, as you can see, a man of some distinction. I have served my country with dignity and pride throughout the most savage and inhuman of conditions. I have seen men smashed to pieces by Russian canon, their limbs splintered and bloody lying in the mire. I have felt the bitter pain this leaves in a man. I have felt it in my mind and I have felt it in my body."

He removed the glove from his right hand, then the left with his teeth. Revealed beneath the black leather were beautifully polished mahogany prosthetics. "As you can see I left the Crimea without my arms." He stared at his wooden limbs without a trace of emotion. "I have grown used to them, for the Cossack's shaska sliced through my flesh fifteen years ago. Yet the agony of his blade biting through muscle and sinew is as fresh to me as if it happened this morning." He looked up from his reverie. "Are you married, sir?" He asked.

"I am not."

He looked back to his hands. "I have never felt the soft flesh of my wife's cheek, nor the warmth of her breast."

"Sir, I am not sure…"

"Can you forge me a hand?" He spoke with a voice barely louder than a whisper.

I opened my mouth to speak, to tell him he was mad and would be better served in Bethlem. Yet, I paused, for what is a human if he is not a machine? Is it not a complex, living machine? My pause gave him cause to look up once again. "If you intend to reply, do so now, or I shall leave." He took a step towards the door.

"Please, sir. Do not leave yet."

In the chill doorway of my workshop, my future had been conceived. I am no magician, and creating a living, feeling hand was beyond my skill. Yet, I knew I could create for Captain Powell something superior to the crude wooden hands he now had; something altogether more fitting for a man such as he.

With my tools and instruments I set about the task with enthusiasm and vigour. The precision of my work was a joy and the dexterity of my fingers was in miraculous unison with my mind.

How could it be then, that the finished model moved with all the fluidity of a gin soaked cripple? The levers fought against each other and the wires stretched and snapped with every minute movement. My ideas were sound, yet the materials were depressingly primitive leaving me with a monstrous abortion, unfit for an animal.

I knew I was better than this monstrosity, better than a simple repairer of machines and yet here I was falling short on a promise. I buried my head in my hands and roared in frustration. How could it be?

I was disturbed from my anger by the sound of tools falling to the floor. I looked up, just in time to see the heels of a thief fleeing through the door.

"Stop!" I cried and jumped to my feet to give chase. What exactly he had stolen I had not yet discovered but he would not get away with my property, of that I was determined.

Within seconds I arrived on the street and found the rogue lying in the filthy gutter, tripped by his own careless steps.

"What have you taken from me?" I demanded. His silence was joined by a callous toothless, sneer which grew slowly across his wretched cheeks.

"You shall come with me then." I grabbed his rancid collar and hauled him to his feet. He smelled of gin and corruption.

I had not yet decided upon his fate as we entered my workshop but until we stepped inside he remained passive, as if accepting of his destiny. This, I quickly realised, was to bring about a relaxed state of mind in me, for no sooner had we stepped across the threshold than his mood changed. He was clearly a man adept in subterfuge and violence for he quickly wriggled free of my hold and felled me with one blow to the temple.

"Now, what've we got 'ere?" He began rifling through my tools and equipment, placing them one at a time inside the lining of his loathsome coat.

Anger, the likes of which I had seldom felt before, slithered through my body and coiled itself about my mind in a poisonous embrace. "Leave my tools alone."

I kept my eyes on him and searched the floor with my hands. He had knocked my hatchet off the bench on his first foray and now my hands found its shaft. I gripped it tightly.

"Leave them now!" I roared. He was so absorbed in the act of theft that he ignored my demand.

I rose silently and without further thought brought the keen blade of the axe down on his arm. The blade had been sharpened this very morning and sliced through the flesh and bone as if it were nothing more than a waxwork model.

Our eyes met and I saw within his soul the fear and confusion my brutal action had induced. I raised the axe again and in a forlorn gesture he raised his severed arm. "Please, sir." His plea went unheard and I ended his miserable life on the edge of my blade.

Disposing of his body was easy, for a great many men of his character are often found floating in the Thames; their bodies wrecked and cut to pieces. Seldom are they claimed, leaving their bloated corpses to sink to the bed of the river like the other detritus. It was in this manner that I dispatched his body. All save for one part, his arm. For in the fleshless bones of his body I found the inspiration to create Captain Powell's hand.

Within a matter of days I had stripped the bones of all flesh and engineered such a work of beauty as there had never been. The perfect harmony of organic and inorganic, of divine and corrupt spliced together in perfect accord.

"And this covering of leather, it is absolutely necessary?"

"Yes, it helps the engineering remain intact and prevents unnecessary damage."

Captain Powell caused the fingers on his new hand to dance inside the gloves. A glimpse of a smile danced across his face and for the first time in our acquaintance he did not appear quite so desolate. I wondered how amusing he would find it if I were to tell him that beneath the leather were the cold bones of a murdered thief.

"Your work is quite remarkable. May I speak of it with my comrades? There are many more like me."

I lowered my head, feeling a flush of pride from his comment. "You may but I would ask for discretion, sir."

Such was the pay for my craft that I was able to generate a healthy income from one or two commissions each year. The bones were easy to come by for the city was full of them. Decaying corpses piled high in the stinking cemeteries with simple-minded, greedy, guardians watching over them. I cleaned the bones and worked them into my designs until they were fit to be used as God intended, once again.

Shrouded in the smug embrace of my success I walked one grey morning to my workshop, passing by the newsagent. It was at once the ghastly headline which aroused my interest. 'Crimea Captain slays wife.' I could not read the article in public view for I knew with a terrible foreboding that Captain Powell was the slayer.

I soon discovered he had murdered his wife by throttling her with his bare hands. The grisly nature of those hands was not recorded, but I knew what they were. His hands had taken on the vile spirit of their donor.

I collapsed to the floor. What could I do? He had yearned to feel his wife's cheek and to stroke her breast. Had he too yearned to feel the brittle bones in her neck fracture? Had I provided him the means to achieve his darkest desire? I would torture myself no longer with these morose thoughts. It was not my concern. I was no more responsible for his actions than I was for the Cossack's shaska cleaving his arm.

The matter disconcerted me though, of that there is no denying. Yet, why should I be surprised at his murderous act? There is no telling what a man is capable of when he is pushed to the brink of his wits, or pressed into a corner as I had been with the thief. Captain Powell was a man like any other.

Powell was hanged on the gallows on a cold December morning. His sleeves flapped limply in the breeze so the world could see his loss.

In the darkness of my dreams, I would hear Powell's pitiful request and feel his skeleton embrace around my throat. His plight, more than that of the thief, was never far from my thoughts and made me lament the loss of my brother even further.

One afternoon, as I sat in quiet reverie, I was disturbed by a female voice. Her clothes spoke of wealth and means, yet her voice was as common as the shrill whine of a workhouse girl. "You can provide this?" She handed me a folded document.

I scanned it quickly and although it was a strange request I nodded my head. "When will you need the first one?" I asked.

"You are not needed for procurement, merely for expertise. You will begin tomorrow." She turned and walked away without further word. Loose strands of hair, the colour of the flames in my hearth, fell about her collar.

Consignments arrived at the door daily and when I had done with them as requested, they were carefully packaged and removed to a destination unknown. I did not ask what purpose my creations served, for I would rather not know. Besides, in this case the purpose appeared to be for entertainment rather than any dark deed.

On the twelfth day I completed the commission, and with the departure of the final crate, sighed with relief. I cannot explain why but more and more I began to think of my brother. The generous payment I received for this commission was sufficient that I would barely have to work again this year. If he were willing, I would part with half of the payment and deliver it to his hands to do with as he wished. Too long had we been estranged and I would not allow the situation to continue.

—

I was restless for the entirety of the grim night hours. I walked to and fro across the cold boards of my room listening to the dull chimes of the distant bells. My brother and I were alike, yet I doubted he had the stomach to do what I had done to succeed. For that reason alone he was destined to fail. Was it my responsibility to ensure his fate was secure? Surely not, and our father would not expect it to be thus. My brother's pride would prevent him from taking the money, of that I was sure, but I would take it nevertheless.

I stepped from my door onto the street and paused in the soft, grey light of the dawn. The air was still and had not yet been violated by the call of a hawker or the clatter of a hoof. It was my favourite time of the day, and despite the bleak nature of my slumber, I felt invigorated by the cool air.

The feeling did not last long for as I reached the city, the fetor grew stronger with each step. There, shrouded in reeking miasma, the dead were laying claim to the land and the living seemed powerless to stop their execrable march.

I finally arrived at the premises and found myself unable to enter. Instead I remained outside staring at the name above the door. 'R.J. Chesterton' and below it in giant golden letters, 'The Gallery of Wax.' How long had it been since I had set foot inside? Too long, and yet now I was here, it seemed like only yesterday. The door was ajar and I pushed it open further. "Richard?" My words echoed around the lobby and returned to me like the ghostly voice from a terrible nightmare. "Richard?" I called again and stepped across the gloomy threshold. In the half-light of the vestibule piles of discarded leaflets littered the floor. Had the business finally failed? Bending. I held one of the papers to my face. 'R.J. Chesterton presents - Ballet of the Bones." It was dated the previous day.

A terrible sense foreboding crept spitefully across my soul. "Richard, it is Frederick, your brother." The building was open, yet clearly not ready for business. I peered along the gallery towards his office. In the gloom a faint light flickered casually, beckoning me on. In times past, the gallery would be full of visitors, even at this early hour. All the displays would have been dusted, oiled and prepared by my father's careful hand.

I took the purse of coins from my pocket and held it in my hand. Judging by the destitute appearance, Richard needed the money more than I. Each one of the galleries was empty, the curtains pulled back as if the show had been cancelled. I reached the end of the corridor and found the source of the light. The final curtain was pulled, but a sliver of light flickered from beneath. Richard was clearly so busy with his work that he hadn't heard me. A steady mechanical sound came from within; the fluid grace of a precision device moving just as it should. "Richard." I called again and pulled back the curtains.

Whatever strength was in my legs deserted me and I collapsed to the floor. My brother was hanging on the gallows beside the skeletal frame of another. The skeleton rose and fell with perfectly engineered grace; it was clear the skill of a master engineer had been involved. It was the work of an engineer who operated outside the restrictive confines of acceptance. I forgot the horror and rushed to my brother; his limp legs were cold and stiff, "What have I done?"

Under the fading light of the gas lamp, I could see two keys. One, my father's and the other my brother's, side by side as the men were in death.

"What have I done!" I roared into the gloom, for the beautiful design was mine. By my own hand I had created the instrument of their demise in my workshop. I looked to my hands. "What have I done?"

Encore

"Is this suitable, brother?" Susanna placed the new poster into my hands. Three skeletons swung from a gallows. Their forms were virginal white against the black abyss of the background.

I drew her close and kissed her sweet, soft cheek. "Perfect, Susanna. Your work, as always is breathtaking. Are they displayed far and wide?"

"From here to Parliament!" The curls of her flaming hair dropped carelessly from her bonnet. She dressed like a lady but had not yet completed the transition.

"Then we must make ready for the audience. I feel, after the success of last night, this may be our finest yet."

We had taken our places and watched as the first Chesterton had arrived. No doubt by now, he had found the final design.

"When can we enter? I wish to watch." My sister enjoyed a performance as much as I.

"We must wait. There is one member of the cast yet to arrive and we mustn't disturb his performance, or get in his way."

I had first come to Chesterton's gallery as a young boy; a young boy captivated by the thrill of a show and in the elegant beauty of performance. Not that I had been granted entry, for according to R.J. Chesterton, his establishment was for gentlemen and ladies of higher birth than mine.

Not even when I returned with a penny and paid my entrance was I allowed entry. No, I was dismissed like a diseased dog with a thump in the ear and kick up the backside. Even the theatres would not turn away a boy with a penny, not even one dressed as I was, in rags and grime. Yet Chesterton was better than they, and could afford to turn away custom, if it was not to his liking.

He was an arrogant man and even in death thought he was better than the rest. Demanding, with all the self-importance of the pontiff, to be buried alone and away from the paupers in their stinking pit.

"He's arrived." Susanna's voice wakened me from my hateful reverie.

"Very good. Now we must wait a little while longer."

I had not yet met the engineer, but Susanna had, and it would be unfortunate indeed to be discovered so close to curtain up. We were both anxious to observe the show but our presence must be timed to perfection to derive maximum pleasure. I took a deep breath of the cool morning air to calm my excited state. For all the wealth of theatrical possibilities, I was happy to be leaving the city; the stench of the dead was tiresome, even for me.

I could restrain Susanna no longer, and after only a few moments had passed, we approached the gallery. I had worked late into the previous night to clear the exhibits, to make ready the stage. The calmness I felt as I winched Chesterton's decaying body into place was a treasured moment of triumph.

"Fear not, Chesterton for your sons will be along to join you soon." The orange glow from the gas lamp made a flickering shadow in the voids of his eye sockets. They were the burning tears of a man in hell.

—

Susanna took my arm and we entered the gloom of the gallery. Papers littered the floor from the previous night and they blew lazily around the hall.

"Hello?" I called. I felt my sister tighten her grip and emit a child like giggle. My heart raced with anticipation for what we might find. What scene had been created for our eyes and ours alone. An agonising scream sounded from the end of the corridor and pierced the charged silence. "Let us see what has become of the Chesterton men. Shall we?"

Susanna smiled and tugged at my sleeve. "Stop teasing me brother."

Each step was deliberate and slow, such as a funeral director at the front of a procession. I savoured the anticipation before we paused at the final curtain. I had provided the props, the cast and the theatre. Now I was anxious to see what they had improvised.

Finally, we stepped in front of the stage and peered in. The spluttering light cast a delicious glow about the stage and threw ghostly shadows about the walls. Two figures were hanging on the gallows; R.J. Chesterton and his son hanging side by side. The skeleton of the hateful man rose and fell against the steady figure of his son; their arms brushing together in a forlorn caress. At their feet, the last of the Chestertons lay in a pond of his blood.

The bloody stump where his arm had been emitted its final utterance of defeat before life was extinguished. By what means he had removed his arm I could not see, but the carving looked to be beautifully and brutally barbaric. It was always such a delightful spectacle to see what a man is capable of, particularly at the point where his mind irrevocably disintegrates. I prayed this magical moment would never lose its charm.

"Bravo!" I shouted and clapped my hands.

Susanna squealed with glee. "How wonderfully poetic!"

"Yes, the entire male line destroyed. It's almost biblical." I stepped onto the stage and gathered up the discarded purses. "We mustn't leave these here, any common footpad could come along and steal them."

As we stepped outside of the dingy gallery a column of visitors had already formed outside. "May we go in?" A gentleman asked.

"Of course, sir. Our finest show yet," and raising my voice I shouted. "And just for today, entrance is free!"

A cheer went up from the crowd as they quickly filed inside. "We should be on our way now, Susanna."

"I should like to hear their thoughts first." Susanna tugged lightly on my arm.

"Very well. The first review and no more." The first shriek was quickly followed by a howl of distress before a perpetual scream filled the air in a fume of fear. In their clamour to see the source of the anguish, the people outside fought with each other to gain entry. It was a beautiful sight to behold.

"Come, we must go now Susanna before a constable arrives." I pulled her to my side and walked away.

"What of the encore, brother?"

I smiled. "Ah yes, the encore. We must visit my friend Thomas, for he has a special place set aside for the Chestertons at Brookfield. I believe it is in a despicable pit with the paupers and thieves. They will be quite at home there."

———

97

The End

SEANCE OF THE SOULS

OF THE

DAVID HAYNES

Séance of the Souls

Contents

A Funeral

Voices in the Parlour

Madame Francatelli

Dinner with Booth

A Séance

34 Bedford Place

The Police

Séance of the Souls

séance

noun

a meeting at which people attempt to make contact with the dead, especially through the agency of a medium.

A Funeral

January 7th 1855

Father died today. A porter found him beneath the iron gates of The Necropolis Railway Station in Waterloo. He thought him drunk at first, such was his slumped and easy manner, but his opinion quickly changed. It was likely he had spent the night there, collapsed and cold in the miserable darkness of the night. Yet, no one could tell us for sure.

He had been a proud man, once. It was his blessed dignity which fought through the twisted abortion his mind had become, and dressed him for his death. The ruined chaos of his once sharp mind had at least afforded him that. His mourning suit was immaculate, save for the greasy mark from the porter's boot and his choice of location had been deliberate, as deliberate as his attire. He chose the site which would convey him as speedily to the earth as the angels to heaven, or his demons to hell.

"Your father has passed, Matthew." My uncle spoke in hushed tones through his grey whiskers. "God save him, for he is in a better place now." I stared at this man, whose countenance was as my father's had been in times before his mind betrayed him. In the days before my mother, his wife, perished. It was now my uncle's duty to safeguard my sister and me. "I will come to live with you. From this day on, you will be known as my son and daughter. You must never forget this day or what has happened."

They brought him home for a while. The dark men in their dark suits paraded him in a parlour chair and took his photograph. My wretched sister and I sat beside him with our hands on his cold, lifeless shoulders. The scent of his hair oil, still faint in my nostrils, could not disguise the odious reek of his decaying flesh. Yet, we sat with him, silent and unmoving as the memento mori captured our family forever.

They laid him out then. Among the flickering candles and the sickly sweet scent of dying lilies, he waited silently for his guests to arrive. When the grim procession had at last departed, we were sent to our rooms. There, under the dark chill of my blankets, I listened to the chime of the clock and waited for the cold touch of his hand. 'Goodnight, my beautiful son. Think kindly of me and pray for my soul.' In the hush of that cold night, the smell of his decaying flesh crept silently through the empty rooms of our home and whispered coldly into my ears.

They took our father and buried him beside mother at Brookwood. There were so many men employed in digging graves, hunched in the misery of the grey morning. It presented a dismal theatre and it was not the time for a vicar to be anything other than brief. The mutes gathered, solemn and drunk, with their black crepe-clad staffs pointing to heaven.

"Why have so many people died today, uncle?" I asked.

He removed the handkerchief from his mouth. "People die everyday, Matthew. Today they are simply putting them all together; in one place."

"So we can find them? So they don't get lost?"

He looked down at me. "So they will not foul the streets and rot with the dogs."

———

The trees were barren and their spindly, finger-like branches could not prevent the wind from whistling around the graves like a furious banshee. My sister clung to my leg with all her might and as we watched my father being lowered into the ground. I heard her fragile voice whisper, "When will we see them again, Matthew?"

"Do not fret my dear Lily. We shall see them again soon and we will be happy together."

My uncle threw soil onto the casket and dabbed his eyes with the white handkerchief. He led us away, through the malevolent sneers of the men digging graves, and onto the waiting train.

"Will father be happier now, uncle?" I asked.

He looked down at me, "I do not know if a man can be truly happy when he has left so much behind." He smiled and touched my head, as my father had often done.

Voices in the Parlour

My uncle had never sought to encumber his life with a family of his own and had made no effort to marry. Yet, he took us in as his own, and made us at once feel nothing less than wanted. Lily seldom left my side and when she did, she returned in such a state of distress that I feared for her sanity.

"You will never leave me, I'll always be with you, won't I? Shuddering and shivering in the grief of her loss she would cleave to my body repeating the gloomy mantra. In the dark night hours she would come to my room and climb in beside me. With her arms draped around me, she would slip silently into her dreams, waking only to scream at the touch of an unseen hand.

My uncle took our father's room as his own. The smell of his cologne still lingered in the air and on the abandoned clothes in his wardrobe. Yet uncle appeared not to notice, or he cared not. He continued with his life as if the death of his brother were nothing more than a passing nightmare; distasteful yet fleeting. The reminder was too great for Lily, who cried and flinched with every touch of his caring hand. She had lost too much, too soon and the wound was deep and permanent.

Somehow, within the maelstrom of our grief, a melancholic equilibrium was reached. It returned our lives to an order not felt since the time before our family was buried in the earth.

Uncle's kindly, yet ambivalent attitude towards my sister and me, was unalike my father's demonstrative personality. His infrequent displays of affection were, I suspected, as much to do with awkwardness as they were do with his true feelings. For I felt that we were both loved.

He appeared confident, affluent and charming on first impression. However, I learned that this was not, in fact, the case. One evening, as my footsteps echoed through the empty rooms of our house, I found myself outside the parlour door. It would not cross my mind to disturb him in the evening, for although he seldom entertained visitors, he preferred not to be interrupted.

"I assure you, Alfred, it is quite the most extraordinary entertainment I have ever witnessed." I spied my uncle through the crack in the door. He was hopping nervously from foot to foot, silhouetted against the flames in the fireplace.

"Quite. And how do you think this feat was achieved?" I could not see the source of the voice but it sounded deep and assured.

"Feat? I do not believe this was a feat, sir. This is religion."

There was laughter then, but not from uncle, who wrung his hands nervously, like a child waiting to be scolded.

"And is this religion of any benefit to society?"

"I believe so. Will you take a brandy with me?" My uncle was as submissive as a lamb to slaughter.

"No, Henry. I have other matters to attend. Bring her here and we shall observe this so called religion for ourselves. I shall see it for myself."

"Very good. I shall make the arrangements and send word."

The sound of his footsteps hastened my retreat but my eavesdropping had left me curious.

In the years before the death of my mother, we had been members of the congregation at St Mary le Strand church. Dressed in our finest clothes, we were pressed into the pews; where we listened to the vicar speak his piece. To my ears, it was as dull as algebra, yet my mother and father listened and took heed of the words. On each and every Sunday, the four members of our family made pilgrimage in such a way, and believed The Lord loved us in return. Yet, with the death of mother, father lost faith in that notion and our visits grew fewer and fewer.

The notion of religion and entertainment being as one was the most curious element of their conversation. I had always found church to be a dreary affair; where entertainment is as far from the experience as heaven is from hell. It was with a deep resolve that I sought to see for myself what my uncle had made reference to.

He did not entertain guests often and so I found it peculiar one night, to hear the muffled exchanges echo up the stairs and into my darkened room. Immediately I leapt from my bed, where poor Lily lay in slumber, and crept to the foot of the stairs. The parlour door was once again ajar, allowing a slice of light from the oil lamp to trickle into the hall. The house was cold and the floorboards chill under my feet, yet I felt nothing but excited curiosity for what I might find and peered into the room.

"Gentlemen, may I introduce, Miss Susanna Fettiplace." My uncle was dressed smartly in my father's Sunday suit. A gathering of four gentlemen stood from a table and bowed in turn to the lady. I could see nothing of her face but her hair, the colour of the flames in the hearth, tumbled down her neck. She too was dressed elegantly, as my mother on her visits to church. There was something about her, an alluring arrogance, which reminded me of my mother.

She sat with her back to the door and the gentleman re-took their seats. They surrounded her as if she were an actress on the stage and they were her audience. Just then, a gentleman appeared with a casket mounted upon a trestle and rolled it into the centre of the room. It was nothing more than a wooden box, but appeared to me as a coffin. She showed no signs of fear and climbed inside without comment. The gentleman spoke; his white hair bounced about his head like fleece. "If I may address you, gentleman? My sister will now sink into a trance. In the darkness of her coffin she will liase with the poor departed souls of your dearest. I give you Spiritualism." He beamed and closed the lid.

Many silent moments passed as I held my breath and waited for something to happen. I had never been to the theatre and father had kept us away from the side street deformities which were so popular amongst his associates. My stomach churned with dread; I had only seen two coffins before and each held the bones of my parents.

Abruptly the silence was punctured by a melancholy wail from within the coffin. In the gloom of the parlour, the men looked on with unease. All save for the silver haired conductor, who crept closer and looked on with glee at their expressions. A series of raps and scratching sounds emitted from within until finally a voice carried forth.

"My brother, is my brother here?" It was a female voice but in the confines of her tomb was both deep and resonant.

My uncle spoke. His voice quavered with fear, or emotion. I know not which.

"Yes, brother I am here. I am here in your house."

Was this my father speaking? How could it be for he was buried deep in the earth at Brookwood? Yet, the voice had asked for his brother and my uncle had answered the request.

The silver haired gentleman lifted the lid with a deliberate flourish and stepped once more into shadow. She rose silently from the coffin and stepped quickly about the parlour as if she were looking for something.

"Brother? I cannot see you, for this medium has my soul but not my eyes. Where are you?"

My uncle took one tentative step forward. "I am here, Edward." He placed his hand on her arm.

"My children, are they safe?" Her voice was feminine, yet uncle appeared not to notice or care.

"Of course. They are asleep and they are loved."

The lady suddenly lurched away from uncle's touch and began a series of violent shudders, which spun her in a circle.

Through the crack in the door, I felt the pressure of her wild, intense expression focus solely on me, but I was powerless to turn away. In the next moment, with my horror mounting, she heaved violently, emitting a guttural sound.

I watched transfixed, as a plume of white vapour crawled from her mouth and spilled onto the rug. It fell in great silken ribbons until it pooled on the floor. I could do nothing but stare; even breathing was too much of an ordeal. As the final vapours gathered at her neck, a ghoulish face took shape and peered out. I rubbed my eyes for this could not be; it could not be real. Yet, I was looking directly into the eyes of my dead father.

She turned to face my uncle again. "That is much better, Edward. Now I can look upon your face."

I did not hear uncle scream, for my own tormented mind drowned out all sound as I fell to the floor in blessed oblivion.

Madame Francatelli

January 12th 1869

"I have no idea how you can bear to do such a thing, Lily. The very idea of it is repulsive." I turned away from my sister. She was decorating the locket with a single pearl, and although the jet was beautiful, what lay inside was utterly distasteful.

"It is no more repulsive than that terrible photograph you insist on holding." She twisted the locket in her hand and held it up for my perusal. "There, quite beautiful. What do you think?"

I did not need to turn and gaze upon her work, for I had seen many such items of her creation. Her mourning jewellery was intricate, delicate and beautiful, yet the lock of hair within was as ugly as the freaks in The Promenade of Wonders.

I looked from the window of our parlour to the snow covered street below. "I am sure it is quite delightful." Instinctively, I reached into my waistcoat and touched the crumpled paper of the memento mori. The picture had lain masked under a deliberate fold for many a year. I had seen my father's cold, dead eyes for the final time when I caught his morbid stare through the crack in the parlour door. I could not look upon that horrifying sight again.

"Why do you find my work so distasteful, Matthew? People find great comfort in knowing their loved ones are beside them."

I took her hand. "It is not your work I find so abhorrent. It is the clamour for all things dead I find so debauched." I took the locket in my hand; the jet was cold to my touch. "It is nothing more than a forlorn memory of something which will never come again."

She took the locket from my hand and slapped my wrist playfully. "Oh, Matthew. You really are the most miserable man I know. Come, we shall go and gaze upon those unfortunate souls on Drury Lane." She took my arm and whispered conspiratorially, "I have heard there is a woman with a beard twice the size of uncle's."

I could not resist her cheerful smile and allowed myself to be led from the house. Lily could bring cheer to the most glum of gatherings. She was too young to remember the passing of our parents, yet when uncle had passed, she was the one to guide me and take my hand. Her playful demeanour concealed a resolve which I did not possess.

"To The Promenade of Wonders!" I called to the driver. We had long enjoyed the passing of an afternoon in the company of the freaks of Drury Lane. Some were nothing more than crude attempts at deception. Others though, were so monstrous that women were forbidden from looking upon them. This notion would enrage my sister to the point where she would be unable to control her feelings. Her vociferous display was often more entertaining than what lay inside but it always resulted in her admission.

Some felt outrage at their performances and claimed society was diseased for their part. Yet I felt no guilt, for where would these souls be employed if not here? Besides, I had heard the monsters were made wealthy from their exhibitionism. Far more wealthy than I.

Lily did not know the meaning of silence, and it was often a source of irritation, but I was glad of the distraction on this afternoon.

"I felt so sad for their loss. You could see the despair in their eyes when they spoke. It is bad enough to lose ones parents but losing an infant must be a terrible weight to bear."

"I cannot imagine. When will they collect the piece?"

"They are sending for it this evening. They seemed such a lovely couple, if not a little old to have a young child. I wonder whether they will have another?"

"I do not imagine losing a child would encourage further attempts." I was eager to change the subject, for death was not a subject I felt inclined to dwell upon. "I shall be eating with Booth at the club this evening." I smiled at her. "He is fond of you Lily, but you know that."

"I don't know how you have the patience to eat with him. He is the most wretchedly dull man in London." She was silent for a moment before continuing.

"Are you still friends with Mr Laurie? Now, he is a wonderful gentleman."

"Laurie is a terrible libertine, as well you know. I would no sooner have you meet him than I would have you meet Lucifer."

She giggled and grabbed my hand. "I do love to tease you, Matthew. You must learn to develop a sense of humour or we shall never find you a wife."

"I do not require a wife." I gazed into the ashen faces of those we passed as the cab rattled along the cobbles towards our destination. Like our uncle, I had never sought the affections of a wife, for what good could come from it? Yet I desired this blessed union for Lily and hoped it would assuage my fear of what would become of her when I too inevitably passed.

We stepped from the cab into the chill of the afternoon. "Where would you like to go?" Lily asked.

"I think I should like to stroll for a moment." The frequent flurries of snow had deterred the usual throng from gathering and I fancied a stroll would clear my mind.

"As you wish." She took my arm.

It seemed that every shop façade had been altered in some way to display a new and gruesome act. The displays seemed to change with the passing of days. No doubt their deceit, once discovered, encouraged their hasty departure.

After a short time Lily pulled on my arm. "A fortune teller!" she cried. "We must step inside. I insist."

I paused and gazed at the tableau indicating what lay inside - 'Madame Francatelli – Fortune Teller.' The crude illustration depicted a woman of exotic appearance staring into a glass ball. A thousand such claims adorned the streets of London, many with a great deal more theatricality than this rudimentary example. I attempted to pull my sister away. "I would much prefer the warmth of The Promenade of Wonders. Besides, where is this bearded lady you spoke of?"

Lily would not be moved. "Oh Matthew, where is your sense of adventure? Come along. We shall see what the future holds for us!"

What had, at one time, been a grocer's or other merchant's shop had been transformed into a dismal oubliette. The flame from the single oil lamp on the table barely illuminated the exposed bricks on the walls.

"Please sit." A woman who bore no resemblance to the illustration on the tableau gestured towards a pair of wooden stools. In the gloom, it was difficult to determine her age but her long departed youth was cruelly exposed.

"My brother and I would very much like our fortunes revealed," Lily said cheerfully. The woman said nothing but stretched her hand onto the table, palm upward over a glass ball. I sighed and placed two pennies in her hand; her flesh felt cold and unpleasant.

She removed her hand and dropped the coins into her skirts. "Who is first, sir?" I could detect the sour aroma of gin on her breath and not a hint of the exotic in her accent.

Without pause Lily leapt in. "I wish to be first Madame Francatelli!" I envied her enthusiasm, for all I felt was disappointment at the lack of comfort.

Madame Francatelli waved her hands above the ball with a lamentable lack of conviction before she locked her eyes on Lily.

"You have the spirit of someone who has lost a great deal and yet I fear there is more to lose. There is grief, there is sadness, and over everything, there is death."

I waited for more but she remained silent and simply stared at Lily who seemed equally transfixed. "What more have you to say?"

"There is no more. This is your fortune," she turned her head and caught my glare, "both of you."

I was astounded by the temerity of this woman. A few mumbled words uttered in the rank darkness of a butcher's shop did not constitute a penny's worth of entertainment. I rose to my feet, pushing the chair noisily backward with my legs. "How dare you take two pennies from me for this! I will see you closed by the…" I felt a tug on my trouser leg. "Matthew, please. I would like to go home now." Her voice was like a stranger's to my ears, fragile and whispered.

I looked down into her eyes, and for the first time since she was a child, I saw distress in her eyes. I took her hand and led her out of that filthy hole. "I should never have allowed it; I am to blame."

By the time we arrived home, the afternoon had diminished leaving only the darkness of the evening behind. I led Lily directly upstairs and into her room. The fire had gone out but I quickly built another and before long the room was lit by the warm glow from the flames.

"Whatever did she mean, Matthew?" She lay on her bed.

"Nothing. She was a common thief masquerading as a psychic. Tomorrow I shall return with a constable and close her deceitful enterprise. She will be in front of the magistrate before the day is out, mark my words." She looked so forlorn, my aggression was not helping. "Why has this troubled you so?"

"I cannot say but I felt her words resonate somewhere within me." She sighed, "Pay no attention to me. I shall rest for an hour, and after the locket has been collected, I shall retire to bed."

"In that case, I shall remain at home this evening. I feel no desire to meet with Booth."

Lily squeezed my hand. "Nonsense. You must meet with him. However else will you manufacture my union with him?"

I was happy to see the carefree expression return once more to her pretty face. "You really are a terrible tease. I shall arrange for him to come for tea tomorrow."

I leapt into the cab. Lily's demeanour had concerned me. She was not prone to sudden swooning, nor had I ever seen her so glum. What was it about Madame Francatelli that had concerned her so? She had spoken the same words to me, yet I had dismissed them with the same disregard as they had been uttered. Still, she had been almost back to her playful self when I left and I consoled myself with that thought.

Booth really was a dreadful bore but he had been my friend since childhood and now I felt obliged to continue our association. The St. James club had been our frequent meeting place since coming of age and was a comfortable location to discuss the trivial matters he so much enjoyed.

After dinner we sat and enjoyed a pipe in the library. "Would it be proper for me to call tomorrow, Matthew? I should very much like to see Lily again." I had not the heart to tell him Lily was not in the slightest bit flattered by his affections.

"Of course. Shall we say three?" I could see the happiness weave across his plump cheeks and for a moment I felt contented.

"She was in delicate spirits when I left this evening. We ventured onto Drury Lane and chanced upon a fortune teller. It was a most disagreeable experience."

Booth threw back his head and laughed. "Why you insist on visiting those charlatans is beyond me." He took a large drink from his brandy glass. "I hoped you would have grown out of it by now, both of you."

"What would you have me do? Sit at home and make trinkets from the hair of corpses like my sister?"

"God forbid! No, you need a pastime. Have you considered politics?"

"No more than I have considered the ministry!"

I cut the evening short, for although Booth became more entertaining the further down the brandy bottle he ventured, I felt anxious for Lily.

The snow had become a miserable rain during the evening and I was contented to be back home again. I had lived there since before mother passed, since before Lily could remember; yet I felt no affection for it. Our family had once been wealthy and employed servants to build fires in the hearth. Not now, not for a long time had this house seen servants. Not since before the time of uncle's ill-conceived ventures, had someone built a fire or hung a coat for us. Yet my sister and I yearned for nothing. Father knew his brother well and protected the house from his foolish hand, bequeathing it to me alone. Perhaps he saw something in me during those precious few years we were together which gave him cause to trust me so.

I seldom ventured into the parlour without Lily by my side. I had seen too much on that damned evening to feel anything other than dread when in it. This night was no different, for without Lily the fire had died, and the room was a silent shroud of darkness. I would not step inside.

I hung my coat and took the lamp she had kindly left by the door before quietly climbing the stairs. An orange glow flickered from beneath her door as I passed. It was not unusual for her to lie waiting for my return. Although she no longer felt the need to hold me through the night, she felt unable to rest until she knew I was home.

"Lily? Booth was asking for you," I knew she would be unable to ignore my taunt. I remained beside the door and waited for her reply, grinning like a schoolboy. "I have invited him for afternoon tea tomorrow. He was very eager." Without reply, I gently pushed the door and stepped across the threshold.

The dying fire cast a retreating glow across the room, barely revealing the bed where she lay. I had seen that crumpled form, lying silent in the darkness of the night many times before, yet as I gazed closer, something about her struck me as unnatural. Her long chestnut hair hung loose and covered her face; it fell over the side of the bed in a voluminous plume. I was suddenly aware of how cold the room was, as if the fire had not been lit at all.

"Lily?" I called softly and stepped toward the bed, "Lily, it is I, Matthew." A feeling of dread had taken hold of my mind, threatening to overcome me. "Lily!" I shouted, caring not if I disturbed every house in Belgravia. I took her cold shoulder in my hand and shook her. "Lily, wake up!"

Her naked shoulder was as cold as our father's flesh when they photographed us together, yet I could not draw my hand away. The locket in which she kept our mother's hair dangled from her neck and dropped over her shoulder entangling her hair. I could see now.

It was not her hair falling from the bed, but blood dripping onto the cold floorboards in a steady unrelenting flow. My legs buckled and I fell onto the bed beside her. I roared into the darkness, "You cannot take her. Not Lily. Not now." Tears ran down my cheeks and dropped in her hair.

I would see her eyes and I would kiss her cheek again. With a soft touch, I brushed at the hair on her face; it was matted and thick with blood. Why had she taken her life as our mother had?

But beneath the tangle of her once beautiful hair was not the face of my sister nor was it the wound of suicide. I gasped and felt the room close about me. Lily's face had gone; her skin had been removed revealing a terrible and bloody mask beneath.

I could not hide my revulsion, for what lay there was my sister no longer. I fell from the bed as I clambered to be free of this ghoulish apparition and as my head hit the floor, I felt the warmth of her blood on my cheek. Who had done this to her, what devil had removed her face? I wanted to shout again, to roar at the cruelty and the pain, yet I could find no air with which to scream.

In the gloom I saw a dark shape in the blood. It was the cherished locket she had been making. I took it in my hands; the cold jet was slick with blood. I turned it over and knew at once the hair inside was not that of a dead infant. It had been removed and replaced with a lock of Lily's chestnut hair. I hurled it into the dying embers of the fire and collapsed once more into the pool of her blood.

Dinner with Booth

Booth accompanied me to Brookwood for I desired no others to be present. They placed her beside our mother and father, beneath the soulless eyes of the marble angel who pointed hopefully to the sky. When the first spade of dirt was thrown onto her coffin I walked away; past the cold iron railings, to The Necropolis Station. I had neither the desire nor stomach to watch any longer.

The police came to my house and left without providing comfort. A lunatic called Lovett had been busy murdering and flaying in the city. He had removed their faces to make macabre masks for his entertainment. Lily was simply one more mask for his collection. This is what the police believed.

Yet, this was not the case, of that I was sure. Lily was no East End ruffian caught up in a mad man's lunacy. The leaving of her locket and hair was proof of that.

"Inspector, I urge you to reconsider. Why would he leave this? He had his prize." I held the singed locket before his eyes.

"Sir, you are considering this man too deeply. He is a lunatic who revels in torment and violence. He left this trinket to torture you further, nothing more."

Lily's hair lay intact beneath the protective shield of jet. What had been beautiful in life was reduced to a clotted mass in death. I would not discard it anymore than I would abandon the memento mori in my pocket. The tips of my fingers were calloused where, in my grief, I had reached into the embers and taken it back.

Lily had scolded me for finding her jewellery so abhorrent, yet here I was, clutching it as if I were a child squeezing a favourite doll. The inspector had left at that instruction and had not returned. Why should he? The case was solved and Lovett was responsible, but I could not rest.

Booth and I stepped onto the train and into the private carriage set aside for mourners. The empty seats reminded me of the same journey I had made with my uncle at Father's funeral. Lily had cried at my side for the entire trip back to Waterloo.

"I should like you to join me for dinner this evening, Matthew. My mother and father are visiting and they will be glad to see you. I will not allow you to be alone this night."

I opened my mouth to speak but Booth held his hand to silence my protest. "It is settled, Matthew. We shall speak of it no more."

I had not the energy or desire to argue. I did not want to be in company but I wanted less to be alone in that house. Besides, Booth's intentions were purely sympathetic and his familiar and cheerful countenance was a welcome sight.

Booth was from a wealthy family with grand connections yet he had never sought to manipulate or use those connections for his own good. He was simply too idle and lacked the ambition which could have provided great fortune.

"We were so sorry to learn of poor Lily, Matthew. She was a fine girl and William here was very fond of her." Booth looked distinctly uncomfortable in his mother's presence.

"Thank you, Lady Booth."

"I trust you have found solace in the words of our Lord."

I had not been inside a church for many years. "I find the church to be somewhat disagreeable these days."

"Oh my dear. You have seen too much sorrow in your life. First your mother, then…"

Lord Booth raised his hand and coughed loudly. "I'm sure Matthew scarce needs reminding of his family, especially not today. We should eat now. Come, Matthew and tell me of my son. What has he been doing with his time? I am quite unable obtain a satisfactory answer."

Booth was not his usual ebullient self at dinner and conversation was strained and sporadic. For my own part I felt thoroughly miserable and at a loss for what to say.

"The congregation at St Mary le Strand has fallen by nearly a third this last year," Lady Booth broke the silence. She had been an ardent advocate of the church for many years. "Why they would turn away so readily is simply beyond me. I fail to see why our so-called middle class are so beguiled by what is nothing more than witchcraft. Two hundred years ago they would all have been burned."

"But mother, we are not living two hundred years ago. For that we should be thankful. It is nothing more than a passing fascination and they will all come back to the church."

"And when will you return, William?" Booth looked away immediately.

"Of what do you speak, Lady Booth?" I asked.

"Spiritualism. There are those who claim to be adept at conversing with the dead and they have formed a religion from it, or at least, they are attempting to. It goes against all the teachings."

"I have heard that term once before, Lady Booth. Forgive me, but I do not wish to hear it again." I met her eyes with my own.

Booth spoke to break the deadlock. "Quite so. It is, as you say mother, nothing more than a passing fascination. Now, who has seen the marvels of my magic lantern?" I blessed Booth, for in his kindly nature, he had diverted the course of the discussion.

Booth's display with the lantern was, at least, distracting. The floating skeletons and phantoms provided unlikely entertainment and for a while my spirits were lifted. Although I felt Booth took a little too much delight in the shrieks of his frightened mother.

When, at last it was time to leave, I did so with a heavy heart. The brandy had warmed my belly but left a sour, unwelcome sensation in my mind.

"I can have a room made up for you tonight and for as many nights as you wish it is yours." Booth grasped my shoulders and looked earnestly into my eyes. I did not need to smell the vapours on his breath for his eyes betrayed how much brandy he had taken.

"My friend," I started, "you have been kind enough to invite me here tonight. I shall inflict my misery on you no longer. In any case, I feel I may have offended Lady Booth."

He clapped my shoulders. "All the more reason to stay. They may depart sooner!"

I laughed despite my mood. "You must offer my apologies for any offence. I shall see you in the club tomorrow?"

"Yes and we shall take a pipe together again."

The cab sped over the cobbles sending the drunks fleeing for the verge. They shambled through the streets like the phantoms on Booth's lantern show. They cared not for the despair of others for the gin they so deeply craved besotted their minds.

*

I spent the night huddled under my blankets with a bottle of brandy. I gained no solace from its warmth, for the more I drank, the deeper into the nightmares I slipped. In the shadows of my tortured mind, I swam in pools of Lily's blood while a flame haired woman and Madame Francatelli looked on and laughed.

By the time the birds announced the arrival of another grey dawn, I languished still within the confines of my brandy induced stupor. I could not rouse myself from the cold and damp sheets of my terror stricken night, for what reason had I to leave the house?

Poor Lily was the most generous and kindly person in the world and had not deserved to die in such terrible circumstances. I should have been at home that night. She had been disturbed by that terrible fraud of a fortune teller and I should have been here to comfort her, as she would have done for me. Yet, selfishly I left her alone. I left her to die. I roared into the half-light and clenched my fists until all feeling was lost. I lay there for a while until I knew what I must do.

I threw back the sheets and dressed quickly. Today I would pay a visit to Madame Francatelli and squeeze her wretched throat until she gasped for breath. She was as responsible as Lovett for Lily's death and I would have justice.

I found a claret in the parlour and consumed it to the very last vapour before stepping onto the street. I was unshaven and unwashed but I did not need to be ready for church to commit what I had in mind. I walked with purpose and glared through the mist at the faces I passed. The stench of the city's rotting corpses filled the cold morning air and formed a sickly medley with the wine on my tongue.

I passed the church of St Mary le Strand had heard the bells toll the hour of ten. The church could rot for all I cared for I knew I would find no solace in the empty words of religious men and their sanctimonious drivel. I pressed on, mindful of the ever-growing stench of death as I descended deeper into the city.

Before much longer, I arrived on Drury Lane, where not a week earlier I had ventured with Lily. Snow fluttered from the sky like feathers from dying angels' wings and awakened the street from its gloomy slumber. Unshaven men huddled and slumped in the doorways, their faces scarred by the pox. They coughed and shivered and muttered their plea.

"A penny, sir? Me bones are chilled."

I ignored them and kept my eyes fixed on the tableau ahead. Madame Francatelli had not fled, as I had feared. Yet as I approached the shop, I could see all was not as it should be. A crimson path cut through the snow and streaked across the road, and into her shop. Here and there, droplets formed bloody wounds in the melted snow. Had someone reached this poisonous fiend before me?

I reached the shop and stared at the tableau. The words were the same and the picture still remained. Suddenly a man appeared at the door. His apron was a vision of blood.

"Can I 'elp you, sir?" He wiped a blood stained fist across his filthy whiskers.

"Where is Madame Francatelli?" I pointed at the tableau for I was unable to take my eyes from him.

"Oh 'er. She left days ago. I'm the proprietor now," A terrible odour crept around his bulk and mingled with the already vile air. "I've just butchered a sow if you're in the market for a leg, sir?"

I turned away for I could feel the burning bile rising in my throat. "Where has she gone?" I uttered.

"No idea. People come and go as the mood takes 'em."

I needed to be away and across the road before my stomach betrayed me. The fumes from his shop were as poisonous as Francatelli's words had been and I had gained nothing by coming.

What sight must I must have looked as I wandered the noisy streets in my anguished state? The bustle of the throng and the chatter of their voices was a distant echo in my mind. I knew not where I was walking but to stop would have been a terrible mistake for I could not have started again.

A distant church sounded midday and I was awoken from the void of my reverie. I paused and looked about my unfamiliar surroundings. Filth was piled in the gutters with the rotting corpses of dead animals. The air was a noxious haze of human waste. If I were in hell, it could be no worse that this spectacle of decay.

I looked for a landmark to raise me from the abyss. I could see none for the buildings loomed over me and covered the sky like a heavy velvet cape.

"Who 'ave we got 'ere then?" A feminine voice called from beyond my view. It was quickly accompanied by the sound of a footfall.

"Well, we don't see your sort round 'ere often. Not unless you want some of this?" I turned to face the voice and was greeted with a sight to match the hellish vista of the street. Dressed in such fineries as would be found in a box at the theatre was a woman of advancing age. Were it not for the thickness of her face paint, I might have estimated her to be close on sixty years of age. She pursed her ruby lips and blew me a kiss. "I'm a pretty sight ain't I?"

I turned my back and walked on.

"Suit yerself."

Lost in the chasm of my thoughts, I had walked many miles and into the East End of the city. It was a place of depravity and violence and I was as out of place as the prostitute would be in the streets of Belgravia.

The cruel monotony of the district was broken as I reached a gaudy display on a shop window. Bright red curtains draped across the glass, and at the bottom, upon a board, was written, 'Gin.' It was not the decadent palace of the Princess Louise in Holborn but the purpose was the same and I stepped inside.

Pressed into the corner was a wooden counter behind which a dissolute hag stood watch. She found a glass and placed it on the bar. Without a word she tipped a measure of clear liquid into the glass.

"I do not believe I have made a request yet." I spoke with more assurance than I felt for this was unlike any place I had ever been.

"This is all there is. No one comes 'ere to talk, just to drink."

I took the glass. It bore the greasy finger marks of the previous user yet I poured the liquor into my mouth and swallowed.

"More." I ordered.

"Where's yer money?"

I slammed a handful of coins onto the counter. "More!"

The afternoon passed in a debauched haze. Men came in and stood beside me, caring not whether I wore a top hat or cap for we had the same purpose. That purpose was to drink. They left while I remained, until I could no longer stand and was pushed from the room like the filthy drunk I had become.

Before me two men fought. Their savagery was appalling, as they beat and kicked each other until the weaker man was felled. His head hit the cobbles with a terrible thump and he was clearly insensible from the impact. Yet, the other man crouched beside him and continued raining blows about his head until his blood ran into the gutter with the other offal.

I slumped beside the door and closed my eyes. Thoughts of Lily with our mother and father swam across my vision in a horrifying carousel of death. In my inebriated state I was unable to vanquish them and joined the other drunken lunatics in their howls of despair.

I do not know how long I remained there but I heard the raucous laughter of those passing by and felt their eyes upon me. The cold of the afternoon crept under my coat and spitefully pinched at my flesh. I hoped the pitiless God of my bleak life would at last show some mercy, and take me to my family.

"Stand, sir. You cannot stay here." I felt a tug on my sleeve.

"I will stay where I fell. I want no help."

"Then you will be up before the magistrate in the morning. Now get up, you do not belong here." The voice was dissimilar to those I had encountered in this district. "Take him under the arms. We shall carry him if we must."

I felt my body being lifted. I gave them no help, yet they lifted me as a child, and dragged my limp body across the wet cobbles; I could not look them in the eye for my shame was complete. I did not care where they took me, for I was already in hell.

"Put him in this chair, then bring him some coffee." I was dropped into a chair and a mug of coffee forced between my clasped hands. The heat from the drink sent a painful spasm through my arms but the warmth was a delicious pleasure. I lifted my head and for the first time looked upon him.

"Where have you brought me, sir?" He was as old as I.

"You are safe in God's house. Drink your coffee and I will return."

I took a sip as instructed and looked at my surroundings. The coffee was laced with molasses and was powerfully rich. If I were truly in God's house, it was unlike any church I had ever entered before. There were none of the familiar pews and the room was scarce any larger than my parlour. Simple wooden chairs lay scattered around the room and in the centre, a crude yet striking crucifix sat atop an altar. Wretched looking creatures filled every one of the chairs, sipping at their sweet coffee. I wondered; did I appear as they did? Abject and without hope?

I rose to my feet. The liquor still held sway over my body but I did not desire to remain in a place dedicated to an entity so pitiless and malevolent.

"You are not fit to step outside yet, sir. Please stay and get warm."

I looked to him again. His face was creased with the expressions of kindness, not of vitriol. "I must go," I muttered.

He placed his hand on my shoulder. "You are not like these others, sir, I can see that, but you have one thing in common; you all possess a broken spirit. Stay and allow me to repair it."

"With God's help?" I hissed the words. "He has sent me to the very abyss in which I now dwell. He does not wish to help."

"Perhaps those who have passed can help you." He smiled and turned away. His answer was simply a statement of belief.

I sat back down. In truth, my legs would not carry me further than the door and the thought of appearing in court was too much to bear. I consoled myself with the coffee and watched him at work.

One by one, the bedraggled guests departed leaving me alone in the church.

"What is the name of this church, sir?" I asked. The coffee had raised my body from the depths, although my spirits still languished in the mire.

"It is a church like any other." He spoke with the voice of a gentleman yet his attire closer matched those of a working man.

"Sir, I thank you for your kindness in bringing me here and away from that miserable street, but please do not seek to make a fool of me."

He held up his hands and smiled. "I do not seek to make a fool of any man. This is the house of God and you are as welcome as any man, woman or child of this earth. If you insist on a name; this is the Spiritualist Church of Spitalfields."

"Then I would be better served in the cell of the police station than here." I stood and made ready to leave.

"You do not belong in the gutter, sir. Seek guidance before it is too late."

I raised my hand to strike him. How dare a spiritualist address me in this manner? What did he know of my situation or my pain? He did not move or flinch, although he was aware of my hand.

"Stop!" A female voice called.

I turned. The strength of the voice belied the diminutive stature of the figure before me. The heavy, hooded cape she wore revealed only a small part of her face, yet from that glimpse I could see there was beauty. "You are forbidden to use violence in the house of God."

I walked toward her. "This is no house of God. It is nothing more than a penny sideshow." I threw a penny to the floor. "Take my penny in payment for your aid."

I brushed past her and opened the door. A gust of icy wind stung my tired eyes halting me on the threshold.

"She is with you," she whispered into the wind. Her words were gone in an instant; buffeted away on a wind which carried the fetor of the slums. I stepped onto the street and under the gaze of an elegant church. Its spire pointed into the gloom like a needle through the dirty linen of the street. I looked to the leaden sky, "Where is your solace?" I asked.

*

When at last I reached my home again, I was exhausted. The words, 'She is with you,' haunted each and every one of my steps. Without Lily, the house had been left empty and cold. No fires had been lit, and no supper prepared. It was desolate and I was alone. I collapsed in my chair in the parlour and stared at the darkened hearth. I did not care what faces might appear from the shadows nor what ghosts might crawl from beneath the boards for I had not the strength to fight them off.

I was not some naïve child upon whom parlour tricks could be played; yet her words struck home and scratched at my heart. Had I been too harsh and dismissive of the kindness imparted by that gentleman? Was my life so utterly miserable that I could no longer treat others with respect? Lily would have berated me for behaving in that manner and she would have been correct. I buried my face into my hands and wept.

A Séance

"I have acted in an appalling manner, quite inexcusable." Booth sat quietly having listened to my account of the previous day's events.

He removed the pipe from his whiskered mouth. "In the circumstances, it is quite understandable." He leaned closer. "Just think of the scandal if you had been up before the magistrate!"

"I dare say nobody would have been in the slightest bit interested."

The glow from the fire transformed Booth's smile into an evil sneer. "Lady Booth would have been absolutely horrified!" He flopped back in the armchair and carelessly wafted an arm above his shoulder. Immediately a boy appeared with a silver tray. "A bottle of port wine for myself and Mr. Napier, I think."

"Have you not listened to my account, Booth? Even the smell of your brandy makes me queasy."

"Exactly. You need fortification. Port is the only answer!" He sent the boy away.

"I shall take one drink with you and one alone." Booth was my friend and was the least judgmental of any of our associates, yet I paused before continuing. "How could it be she knew of my loss and the loss was of a woman?"

"Nothing to it. Why else would a gentleman like you be found as a common drunkard in the gutter? There is only one source of such misery in this world and that is the loss of a woman. It does not take a conversation with the dead to see that is exactly what caused your malaise."

"Perhaps you have a point."

"Of course I have a point! Ah here comes the port."

Why was it then that I found myself in a cab rattling along the cobbles towards Spitalfields in the murky glow of the gas lit night? I had tried to convince myself that I had nothing more than an earnest apology in mind; but that was not the case. I knew I would never be able to rid my mind of her words unless I discovered the meaning for myself.

The driver had never heard of the church and in the darkness the streets looked as unremarkable as any other. Men lurked in doorways and the prostitutes plied their trade. The sots fell bleeding and drunken in the gutters while dogs fought over bones picked clean. Screams and cheers punctuated the dreary hum in equal measure. Wherever God was, he had not been here for a very long time.

"There!" I called, and thrust my cane into the roof of the cab. The spire of the church, which had greeted my departure from the spiritualist's parlour, provided a useful landmark.

I had taken no notice of the door on my exit but now as I looked upon it I could see a simple wooden crucifix had been nailed on it. In comparison to what lay across the street it was a poor relation indeed.

The door opened under my pressure and I stepped inside. The interior of the church, if that was what it was called, was as cold as the street outside. Three small windows high on the wall allowed the insubstantial glow from a distant lamp to limp inside.

"Hello?" I spoke quietly into the void. When no answer came I walked further into the room. How this could be termed a church was beyond me. Where were the golden chalices or the bejewelled crucifixes of St Mary le Strand? There were none and the room smelled strongly of cheap brandy and gin. I had come to the wrong place if I expected answers of the divine kind and I turned to leave.

"I trust you are in better spirits tonight?" The sound made me start, though I recognised the voice from the previous day.

"I cannot see you. Please step closer." I urged.

"Of course. I apologise." His kindly face came in to view.

I removed my hat. "It is I who must apologise, sir. I fear I was not at my best yesterday and that is why I am here, to say how very sorry I am."

He offered his hand and although our standings were clearly established I took it. "There is no need for apologies here. You were clearly troubled and I was only too happy to offer any assistance I could. I am John Collins and I am very pleased to make your acquaintance."

His charming manner was disarming. "Matthew Napier."

He released his grip. "Now, what can I help you with this evening. You certainly haven't travelled this far to simply apologise."

"You do not know my character Mr. Collins so do not presume to educate me on my intentions."

"I do not presume anything. I simply observe."

"And what is it you observe?" My hostility was beginning to show.

"I see a man who is lost. A man who does not know which way to turn and is looking for answers. Nothing more."

His words rang an awful truth within me and I could not utter a word.

"I cannot provide the answers, Mr Napier but there are members of my congregation who may, if they so choose."

"There is a congregation who worship here?"

"Yes, like any other church. I shall find my sister; she will be able to direct you better."

"Your sister?"

"Yes, Anna. You met her briefly yesterday, at the door. She spoke to you I believe?"

I nodded in agreement, for she was the purpose of my visit. "Is she here?"

"She is currently engaged but you are welcome to wait. I shall bring a lamp." Collins departed through the doorway from which he had appeared.

As he left, I fancied I heard voices coming from beyond the door. My curiosity was piqued by this odd arrangement and so I followed his footsteps and peered around the door. A narrow corridor awaited on the other side. It was oppressively dark with an odour of dampness dominating the air, but at the far end, a sliver of light crept along the floor.

"Hello, Collins?" I cocked my head and listened for a response. No voices answered my call but instead the melancholy timbre of the flute snaked through the darkness to my ears. The haunting melody caressed my body and took my neck as a silken scarf, drawing me toward its source. 'Come with me,' the music whispered and urged me to the heavy curtain which obscured my sight of what lay beyond.

I could not help myself, nor did I want to, and brushed it aside. I had been seduced by the light kiss of the harmony and as my intoxication reached its zenith, I stepped into a world like no other.

The bland and soulless church seemed like a weak apology next to what lay before me in the lavish golden light of a hundred candles.

Had I not been in a supposed house of God I might have thought I had stumbled upon a bordello, such was the extravagant décor. My eyes flicked rapidly around the room waiting for someone to address me, someone to notice me.

There were a dozen people in the room, reclining on luxurious leather settees and velvet crimson chaises, yet, none of them even looked up. They too were in rapture at the wonderful melody drifting languidly amongst them.

My eyes stopped on the musician and even though I had only set eyes on the woman once before, I knew it was Anna. I cannot say how long I remained on the threshold but when the music ended I could not move. Not even when Anna opened her eyes and caught my gaze.

"Mr Napier?" John Collins spoke but I could not turn for I was under Medusa's spell, albeit a delightful one.

"Sorry, Collins. You were gone for so long I suspected something had happened."

I expected a reproach for blundering into a gathering which was clearly a private matter; but there was none, just a smile.

"Well you must come in and join us. My sister always starts the evening off by playing the flute. Come, I shall introduce you properly." I nodded politely to the other guests as I crossed the room but they were all engaged with each other and appeared to care nothing for my impromptu appearance.

"This, Mr Napier is my sister, Anna."

"You play beautifully. What was it called?" The capacity of my senses was being tested.

Anna held my gaze for a moment without replying. Her stare was cold. "It is from Dance of the Blessed Spirits by Gluck. Has your temper improved, Mr Napier?"

Her tone was one of amusement rather than reproach. "Yes, I'm afraid I owe you and your brother an apology."

"And I am sure John has told you the apology is unnecessary. What brings you here tonight, Mr Napier?"

"I wanted to…" I paused. Why exactly was I there? What did I hope to gain? "I wanted to ask you what you meant when you spoke to me at the door yesterday?"

"Yes. I too must apologise for my rudeness. I intended no harm, Mr Napier. You are aware of our movement?" Her expression had softened.

"I have experienced spiritualism only once and it was not pleasant, but yes, I am aware, if somewhat ignorant." I refrained from voicing my true opinion on the subject.

"I spoke only what I knew to be true when you brushed against me."

"True? Of what truth do you refer? She is with me. That is what you said."

"A female walks beside you Mr Napier. I do not know her name and I do not know her purpose but she was there."

"What did she look like?" I blurted out, unable to hide my impatience.

"I could not see her face. It was nothing more than a feeling," she sighed. "I do not know how to explain it yet. My journey has only just begun, unlike some of our other guests who are vastly more experienced." She took me by the arm, "I shall introduce you to them."

She led me across the room to a couple enveloped in deep discussion. Anna spoke without waiting for them to turn.

"Mr Napier, may I introduce Louis Lightfoot."

The gentleman turned and nodded sending his white hair into a merry dance. "Delighted to make your acquaintance. I am very happy we have more people here this evening. Last week there were only three of us and it was a terrible bore." His speech was eloquent but betrayed the tone of a common man.

He turned and addressed the woman standing beside him. "May I introduce my sister, Susanna Lightfoot."

I turned my attention to her and gasped. Flaming hair fell about her neck in loose coils. I had seen that hair before yet it could not be the same woman for she had not aged a day.

"Are you well, sir? You look washed out."

I gathered my senses quickly. I must have been mistaken. "Yes, quite well. It has been a difficult time, that is all." I turned my attention back to Mr Lightfoot for I could look on her no longer, "I have come only to speak with Miss Collins, here. I shall intrude no longer. Good evening."

I turned away and took a step to the door. My heart was beating a terrible rhythm and it threatened to push through my ribs.

"Lily is with you."

It was the voice of Miss Lightfoot. I turned quickly and glared at her. She smiled as she spoke.

"Mr Napier, your darlin' sister is standing beside you as we speak. Her chestnut hair flows in a great cascade to her waist. She wears an exquisite locket around her neck, and within it a lock of her mother's hair is kept."

I felt the strength in my legs depart but I was determined not to fall, not in this room full of strangers. I felt a hand on my arm. "Do not be concerned, Mr Napier. Your sister is with you and that should be of great comfort, not horror. In his wisdom God has bestowed upon Miss Lightfoot a great gift and with that gift she gives relief to those in need." She led me to a crimson chaise and urged me to sit.

I felt like an automaton being manipulated by the craftsman's hand. I had neither the spirit nor wits to resist. "You must take a moment. I understand this is a difficult thing to accept but the spirits of our loved ones are amongst us and they yearn to be heard. There are those like Miss Lightfoot who can hear souls as if they were standing beside them. There are those like me who can only sense them and there are others like you who resist the very thought of it. Open your eyes, Mr Napier and you will see them." Miss Collins walked away leaving me alone on the chaise.

A copper haired spectre from the past had materialised and was standing in this very room. I could not recall her face in very much detail but I was sure it was the same woman. I kept my eyes fixed on her, trying to regain a memory which had been interred for so long.

I was not permitted sufficiently long to complete my recall, as one by one the candles were snuffed. It left a solitary flame to light the space. In silence, the guests took their seats around a table in the centre of the room. A loaf of bread lay between them.

"We must hold hands now." The group followed Susanna's direction.

The entire group spoke as one. "Beloved Robert, we bring you gifts from life into death." The chant was repeated and then there was silence.

I had not come to be part of this but I could not leave, for the mounting horror I felt, conspired with curiosity and left me utterly enthralled.

The silence was broken by a number of sharp raps on the table.

"Is this Robert? One rap for yes, two for no." A rap sounded again followed by a loud, feminine gasp.

"Thank you Robert. Your darling, Rose is here. You may speak directly to him now, Rose."

"Robert? It is me Rose," a thin voice called out in the darkness. "Are you happy on the other side?"

Two knocks were accompanied by a sharp intake of breath.

"Has the pain diminished?"

There followed two knocks and a piercing shriek from Rose.

"I must help him! Poor Robert died in agony and now his spirit is trapped in eternal pain. What must I do?"

The knocking became louder, and under the weight of those present, the table rocked, sending the guests crashing against one another. The room was a cacophony of tormented wails and cries, but in the midst of the furore, I caught the sound of a low cackle. It was a base sound and if I were inclined in such a way I might have thought a witch was present.

As abruptly as the tumult commenced, it abated and all was still again. Save for the occasional sepulchral moan, the room dropped once more into silence.

I shuffled uneasily on the chaise. In my mind this was nothing more than a simple trick played on a poor woman who needed reassurance and comfort. Instead she had been cast deeper into her own torment at the whim of a cackling witch. It was utterly deplorable and I felt contempt for this charade which had been carried out in the name of some twisted religion. I could watch it no longer.

As I stood, a terrible roar came from Miss Lightfoot. It did not seem possible that such a guttural sound could come from her, yet it did. In the inadequate light, I saw the silhouette of her figure arch backward and brace itself rigidly in the chair.

"Matthew!" she screamed.

I remained where I stood, unable to move.

"Matthew! My brother, where is my hair? What have they done with it?" Miss Lightfoot stood and walked toward me. Her face was a twisted, snarling abortion.

"Stop this! Stop this now you witch!" My voice betrayed the dread I felt and carried none of the resolve I desired.

"Matthew, it is I, your sister." She came ever closer, twirling the amber curls of her hair carelessly between her fingers.

"You are not Lily. This is an evil trick. I demand you stop." But I could not turn away and I could not move.

She screamed and in a gasping whisper continued. "There were two of them, Matthew. They took my hair." Something fluttered before my eyes and instinctively I reached out and took it. Before I opened my fist, I knew what it was. In the gloom I could see clipped strands of dark hair. I lifted them to my nose and smelled the sweet scent of Lily's perfume.

"It cannot be," I whispered.

I felt the soft touch of hand on my cheek. "My face, Matthew. What have they done to my face?"

I looked up, and in the dismal light, saw my sister's face; bloody and wrecked, staring back at me.

"It is I, Matthew. Your darling sister." A sneer appeared upon her deformed and bloody lips.

The strength in my legs deserted me and as I collapsed, a faint whisper fell upon my ears. "I am with you, Matthew."

*

"Wake up, Mr Napier." A gentle voice raised me from the dark abyss of my unconscious mind.

The last sight I had seen was that of poor deformed Lily and I feared seeing her face again.

"Come back to us now." The voice softly urged again.

I opened my eyes slowly, knowing what horror awaited me. Instead I looked upon the soft features of Miss Collins smiling down at me. Behind her, the room was once again awash in candlelight.

"Bring him sweet coffee, John. Steady there, Mr Napier, you had a nasty fall."

"Where is the witch?" I spoke with more reassurance than I felt.

"Oh, Mr Napier. Miss Lightfoot is no witch; she is a medium. She left with her brother a few moments ago. She was most concerned about you and fretted that if she remained it may cause you more distress."

"My sister, she looked…" I could not form my thoughts coherently.

"We shall talk about it later, if you wish. For the moment we must bring you to the chaise and allow you to gather your wits. Here." She slipped her arm under my shoulder and helped me to sit.

"She is a deceiver." I became aware that the entire room was empty save for Miss Collins and myself.

"She has been called that before, but it is simply not true. There are those who seek only to console when it is not the truth. Miss Lightfoot tells the truth and it is often unpalatable."

"I asked for nothing. I did not come seeking consolation or anything else."

"I believe you did, Mr Napier. You came here tonight to find something you have lost. Hope."

"But I did not come to see such horror or pain. Did you see her face? It was the twisted face of agony. This has left me in despair for poor Lily."

She placed her hand on my shoulder and looked on me with kindness. "I do not claim to have the skills of Miss Lightfoot and do not see what she sees. But, I feel something different. I feel warmth and happiness and love."

"Her face though, did you not see her face?"

"I only saw Miss Lightfoot and nothing more."

My mind was a vicious tumult of chaos. Was this where madness began? When a man has lost everything he loves, is this when the hellish creatures of his nightmares take hold of his mind and drag him screaming down to their lair?

"Take this for your nerves," Collins pressed a glass into my hands. "It will be of more benefit than coffee."

I took a sip. The warming liquor flowed through my system, spreading calm as it went.

"People often feel this way on the first occasion. It will pass." He smiled down at me.

What had gone before was truly abhorrent, yet as the brandy slipped easily through my body, something else was starting to take hold. In addition to my revulsion, I started to feel a grotesque fascination for Miss Lightfoot. She was a witch and a deceiver but how had she managed to conjure up such a startling display? How had she known about poor Lily's locket? How had she…

"What is it, Mr Napier?" Miss Collins asked.

Was it possible that I had stared into the face of my sister's murderer? Surely this could not be the case. "Nothing. I am still quite shaken by the events of this evening. Would it be possible for me to come again? To see Miss Lightfoot, personally?"

They both looked pleased with my request, yet they did not know the dark questions which lurked in my mind.

"Of course. You may prefer a private consultation? I would be quite happy to bring them to your address."

"Them?" I asked.

"Yes," replied Miss Collins, "they seldom travel alone."

I handed her my card. "I shall await their response." I felt my composure returning as my mind focused on the grisly possibilities.

"I feel much better now, although I am quite exhausted. I have solicited too much of your kindness already and so I must return home."

I heard their voiced entreaties for me to stay a while longer but my mind was already somewhere else. It was a place where justice was done on my sister's murderers, justice by my own hands.

34 Bedford Place

In spite of the comforting warmth of a further brandy taken at home, I found sleep once again difficult to come by. My head swam with question after question regarding Miss Lightfoot and her brother. They had been called something else, I was sure, when they visited my uncle those years ago. What was their surname back then?

Her knowledge of my sister and her demise was startling but it was no magic trick. It was the deceit of a murderer or someone close to the murderer and I would have my answers. Was Miss Collins too involved in this appalling scheme? It seemed inconceivable that she would be. Both she and her brother appeared to be kind and genuine, without the need for deception. Yet their very presence was disconcerting, especially since Miss Collins insisted she was gifted with the power, albeit of a gentler and subtler guise. In that respect, her claims were less absurd.

The police would hear nothing of this. They had already got their killer, Jonathan Lovett, and were convinced of his guilt. Besides, apart from her knowledge, which she could easily claim came from beyond the grave, what evidence was there? No, it was simple enough, I would have to discover the truth for myself.

Fettiplace! That was the name he used to introduce his sister on that terrible night.

When, finally I fell asleep, my dreams were vivid and base; I dreamed of Anna Collins. She played Dance of the Blessed Spirits on the flute and danced naked above the rotting corpses of my family.

The music washed over their bodies and re-animated them. My mother and father clung to each other and danced a staccato waltz in their ragged clothes, whilst my sister and uncle laughed and cheered. When the dismal melody finally ended, they collapsed in a jumble of ruined bones and melted back in to the earth. 'Come to me,' Anna urged, 'come and be my lover.' She lay on the earth above their heads and waited for me to lie with her.

*

The morning passed in solitude until a ringing of the doorbell disturbed me. A young boy who appeared to be recently escaped from the workhouse greeted me.

"Well?" I asked, for he stood in silence.

He said nothing and handed me an envelope, which had it not been for the dirty finger marks, was of remarkable quality.

I started to close the door.

"I was told to wait for your reply, sir."

I closed the door and opened the envelope.

Dear Mr Napier,

My sister and I apologise most vehemently for causing you distress last night. We would be delighted to attend you this evening, at your home, and will happily forgo the usual fee in recompense for your distress. Miss Collins will accompany us.

The messenger will bring your reply.

Yours faithfully

Louis Lightfoot.

The handwriting was impeccable and the notepaper of the highest quality, yet there was no return address. I quickly wrote my reply and took it to the boy outside.

"From where did you bring this message, boy?"

"I'm not to say, sir."

I took a penny from my pocket and gave it to him. "You may speak to me. I will not say a word."

"Thirty-Four Bedford Place in Bloomsbury" He took the penny and ran off before I could ask him anything further.

I was unfamiliar with the address but Bloomsbury was a respectable district filled with the satisfied bellies of clerks and their burgeoning families. In knowing their address, I felt content that should I require the services of the police, I would know where to send them. In my response I had asked for the party to arrive no later than eight o'clock. I would hear her séance and make a decision on my next step after that. It would not do to underestimate them or their intentions.

*

In perfect harmony, as the mantel clock struck the hour and conducted its perfunctory chime, the doorbell rang, signalling the arrival of my guests. I had decided my manner would be warm and welcoming. I did not want to arouse their suspicions, although if my conjectures were correct, they had been inside my home before, on two occasions.

Miss Collins stood at the front. "Miss Collins, thank you for making the arrangements in preparation for this evening." I smiled and bowed my head.

"My pleasure, Mr Napier. Would you do me the honour of calling me, Anna? I would be much happier to be addressed like that."

"And we should very much like to be addressed as Louis and Susanna!"

Fettiplace called from outside where he stood with his sister.

"Come in, come in. It is a cold night and we should gather on the step no longer than is necessary. If we are all in agreement then, I am Matthew." It was not in my nature to be on Christian name terms with those of a lower class, yet tonight was an exception and suited my purpose.

"Allow me to take your coats and please go through into the parlour. I have made a fire and the room is warm."

Anna handed me her coat and smiled. Immediately I recalled the dream of her naked body. She held a long case in the other hand.

"You have a wonderful home, Matthew."

"I'm afraid it is too large for me now and much too cold!" I followed them into the parlour. Louis and Susanna looked about the room as if studying the design. I had lit only one candle but it sat beneath a great mirror on the mantel and the reflection exaggerated its size.

"Louis? I believe we have been here on a previous occasion."

"Yes, there is something familiar about it." Louis turned to me, "Have you lived here very long?"

"All of my life." I replied, a little curtly. I was unprepared for their admission.

"Well, we have visited a great many houses in your career. Have we not Susanna?"

———

Susanna nodded but said nothing more on the subject.

"Would anyone care for a drink before we begin?" I asked with as much courtesy as I could muster.

"I should prefer to begin, if that is agreeable Matthew? Do you have a suitable table?" She cast her eyes about the room, "Ah yes, that will be perfect."

Anna put the flute to her mouth and played the same lingering melody I had heard the evening before. I was again reminded of my lurid dream and turned away from her in shame. After she finished playing we sat around the occasional table Lily and I used to play whist on.

"Can you feel it, Susanna?" Anna asked.

"Feel what?" she replied dismissively.

"There are a number of spirits here, with us. I cannot explain it but it is how I feel."

"Please allow my sister to begin. She needs peace to commune with the spirits."

There was something in the manner of their response to Anna which was cold and irritable, as if she were a hindrance.

"Do you have anything of your sister's with you?"

"I have only this." I placed the damaged locket containing her hair onto the table, "The hair inside belongs to her." I tried to examine her countenance in the dark but she remained impassive. She turned it in her hand before placing it on the table.

"We must all join hands." Susanna closed her eyes and inhaled deeply. Above her head, her deformed, flaming shadow flickered in the draft.

"Who is it you wish to commune with, Matthew?" she asked.

"My sister, Lily." I felt pressure from Anna's grip on my hand.

"We are seeking, Lily. Come Lily and communicate with us." There was silence for a few moments.

"Will you all join me in repeating those words." Susanna spoke quietly.

We all spoke as one. "We are seeking Lily. Come Lily and communicate with us." Silence followed but as I started to relax, the calm was shattered.

"I am in purgatory." Susanna screamed.

"Lily?" Despite my intentions, I felt compelled to ask.

"Yes, Matthew it is I." Susanna smiled at me with her eyes still closed and in the half-light her face was monstrous.

I had planned my first question to bring about a reaction from the siblings. "Who murdered you, Lily? The police say it was a man called Lovett but I do not believe them."

Susanna's eyes flicked open. "It was the couple Matthew. I allowed them entry to view the locket. They forced me upstairs and, and…" A terrible howl arose from her, "Such pain, such terrible agonising pain. I screamed for you brother. I screamed for you until the blood ran down my throat and coated my teeth. Why did they do this? Why did you let them do this to me?"

I had vowed to myself that I would retain control of this situation but now the moment was upon me I was powerless. This woman was too skilled in the corrupt act of emotional deception for my naïve resolution. She had found the exposed flesh of my weakness and was taking nibbles with her razor edged teeth.

"I am sorry, my poor sweet sister. I have let you down; I deserted you in the time of your greatest need. Can you tell me the names of those that did this to you?"

Susanna brought her fist down onto the table with a violent crash sending the locket somersaulting into the fire. "Take that locket away from me! It has my hair inside. You must burn it!" I watched in tortured anguish as the locket slipped beneath the savage amber ripple of flame and vanished.

"No!" I shouted and jumped to my feet. I felt resistance from Anna's grip as she tried to prevent me from leaping into the fire to reclaim the locket. I looked down and saw the dark pools of sadness welling in her eyes.

"You must leave it to burn, Matthew. You should not cling to an item so drenched in pain and blood; leave it be." Her voice quivered with emotion and I could not answer for the strength of my feelings would betray me. The flames licked and spat as they devoured my sister's bloody hair sending an acrid smell into the room.

"Mother is here with me, but it is so dark, we cannot find Father. There are foul creatures here with us. Help us please, Matthew."

I took hold of the table and tipped it over sending brother and sister tumbling onto the floor. "You will leave my house now!"

Louis got to his feet first. "I am quite sure there is no need for this! My sister is respected and this behaviour is abominable." He helped Susanna to her feet.

Anna spoke quietly; at first it was no more than a whisper in my ear. "Lily did not say any of those things, Susanna." Then as if she had been courage she spoke much louder, "Why would you say that to him?"

"This is preposterous! How do you know what his sister said? You are nothing more than a pathetic dreamer." Louis spoke and for the first time, I could see the fire reflected in his dark eyes.

Anna shrank back, her courage gone. "I just know."

Susanna glared at me. "Your sister is in pain and she blames you for it. I know this and you should know it as the truth and not some deluded fantasy of happiness. She turned her eyes to Anna, "And you should be wary of the steps you take. Not all spirits are the happy ones of your church."

"Leave her be!" I shouted. "I have asked you both to leave. Should I make my request more forceful?"

I watched as Louis sank his hand deep into his trouser pocket. I took a step backward, expecting him to withdraw a blade or other weapon. He saw the look of fear on my face and gave me a brief glimpse of his teeth in return. He withdrew a handkerchief and dabbed at his forehead.

"Come, Susanna. We shall leave Mr Napier to the misguided fantasies of Miss Collins." He bowed his head, "We shall see ourselves out. Good evening."

We stood side by side and watched them leave.

"They have deceived us both, Matthew." Anna was clearly distressed.

I turned to her. "You can hear something she cannot? What is it you feel, Anna?"

"I do not know, but I it is not as Susanna says. This house is filled with sadness, Matthew. The very air is oppressive and unhealthy. Can you not feel it too?"

I shook my head. "It is my home and has always felt this way. You should take a drink to steady your nerves and I will take you home."

"I should like that."

In truth, I too needed the calming influence of brandy before I could step out of the house. We sat together in the parlour and talked of matters which inevitably led to those of a morbid nature.

Like Lily and me, Anna and her brother had been left without the influence of their parents from an early age. Unlike us, they had not been blessed by wealth but were raised by their mother's family. It came as no surprise to learn that those who raised them were devoutly religious. Anna and John's current beliefs had caused an unfortunate separation of the family which she regretted most deeply. It was though, a belief which she would not be swayed from.

When at last a pause silenced the conversation, I again recalled the sordid details of my dream.

"I must deliver you safely back to your brother. It is getting late."

As the bells struck midnight I left Anna with John at the door to her church.

"May I call on you tomorrow? There remain a great number of questions still unresolved and would be glad of your company. If your brother is content to allow you?"

Anna smiled. "Of course, John is happy with that, aren't you brother?" Collins simply smiled and nodded. Anna continued. "I have no business to attend tomorrow and would be happy to help answer any of your questions."

*

"Back to Belgravia, sir?" the driver asked.

"No, I wish to go to thirty-four Bedford Place now please."

"Very good, sir."

The cab sped across the cobbles and once again I travelled the streets of London in the silence of the chill night.

I had not thought what I would do when I arrived at the address. Indeed, the notion to go there had only reared its head after leaving Anna. Even so, as I jumped from the cab I was determined to see the dark secrets they kept locked in their home.

Bedford Place was as I had expected, a quiet and respectable location in which to keep a home. The burgeoning middle class of London could not afford to live in splendour but they could afford to live comfortably and with elegance. As I looked upon the bland walls of their houses, stretching four storeys into the night, I envied those inside, for they possessed everything I did not.

Number thirty-four was as unremarkable as any other, save for one adornment. The slim sentinel of the lamp post with its hazy flame threw a gloomy light over their door. Black crepe tied with white ribbon lay upon the bell knob.

It was a sign that the dread visitor had entered the lives of those living here and taken his prize. Could the messenger be mistaken with his knowledge of their address? It was possible, yet something inside told me this was where I should be.

Neither Louis nor Susanna had displayed the usual adornments or attire of death but their house clearly did. I paused at the foot of the steps. I had indeed fallen too far if I sought to confront them here in their moment of grief.

I turned to walk away, to find a cab to speed me home. My mind was disturbed by the death of my sister and by the tricks of their séance; their evil, debauched deception. If they wished to amuse themselves in the abyss, I would not be a willing playmate.
I turned back. Neither would I be used like a child's doll and left to rot in the maelstrom of my tortured mind. I mounted the steps quickly and pushed aside the crepe wreath. I pushed the bell knob but it uttered no sound, instead the door swung slowly in, allowing me access.

"Fettiplace?" I called into the shadows where the street lamp could not reach. Silence greeted my call.

"Is anyone at home?" I called again and garnered the same response.

I found myself with choices to make, but standing on the threshold as I was, I did not consider my options and stepped hastily through the cheerless veil.

The house was as cold as my own and felt equally bereft of life. I waited and clung to the last semblance of light as it fell through the door. There, I listened for a voice, or the sound of footfall to usher me out onto the street, but none came.

The hallway was much smaller than my own. No hat or coat stand stood on guard and a set of stairs encroached on the space. I looked upward and in the darkness spied a sliver of light etching a sombre line across the boards. I was instantly and gravely reminded of the night I found Lily; the sight of her ruined face and the feel of her blood, clammy on my fingers.

"Hello! The door is unlocked." I shouted much louder this time but the only reply was a dull echo.

The feeling I held in my mind was confusion and disquiet. Yet why could I not leave that house? Why did I remain rooted like a tree to the spot? It was certainly not in my nature to enter someone's house uninvited like a burglar, but I felt compelled to remain and to see what played out before me.

I took the stairs slowly at first, listening for the fall of a human foot, but as my confidence grew, so did my speed. Upon reaching the top I paused. The light emanated from beneath a closed door

"Fettiplace, I will know the truth!" I called again and pushed the it open.

Inside, the room was bathed in candlelight and in the hearth a great fire burned with freshly lit intensity. But it was not the candles, nor the fire upon which my eyes were fixed. It was the trestle standing beside the fire, upon which balanced a small coffin. Death had indeed paid them a visit and in recent times too; for there was none of the mellifluous odour which added one to the number of mourners.

The coffin was sized for an infant and I had no desire to look upon the poor thing. A myriad of photographs stood beside the coffin, all in beautiful and elaborate frames. Had the death of Susanna's infant so warped her mind that she felt the compulsion to hurt others? I took a photograph in my hand. It was nothing more than the infant lying in a crib, either asleep or dead, I could not tell.

There were many others of a similar nature, yet the differences were subtle and disturbing. The infant's features became more and more sunken, charting an inexorable decay. How terrible a thing to gaze upon.

It seemed strange that I could find no images of Susanna holding her baby. There was only one photograph where the infant was in company with others. A young boy and girl posed with the infant upon their knees. Unlike the others, the baby's eyes were open, and a thin smile danced upon its lips. Both the boy and girl sat expressionless and dour. Who were they?

A final image sat upon the mantel. It was framed with golden flourishes and scrolls which would have suited a gallery masterpiece. The photograph had been carefully posed and in the image were the bodies of four figures. A lady sat with a swaddled infant in her arms and huddled at her feet were two children. She was beautiful and elegant but looked sad somehow, as if she felt the weight of a terrible fate bearing down on her. Behind them all stood the suited figure of a gentleman. I held the photograph closer to see their faces, but the gentleman's face had been obliterated. Was this their father? What grave act had he committed to deserve this destiny?

If the infant in the coffin was the same child from the photographs, then the corpse should be rotting in the earth, not sitting in a drawing room shrine. I could restrain myself no longer and lifted the lid.

A tiny skeleton lay in the chamber. It was wrapped in bright and fresh linen.

"I am armed, show yourself!" A voice boomed from the hallway beneath.

Terror streaked through my veins like venom and rendered me lifeless. This was not something I could explain through a simple error or a misguided offer of help. I had come here in the darkness of the night and forced entry, it was as simple as that. I looked about the room for an object to conceal my presence, but apart from the coffin, there was nothing.

Footsteps sounded on the stairs. "You will be sorry for your trouble!" Female laughter sounded after the threat.

As my fear threatened to overwhelm me I noticed a door in the darkened corner of the room and ran toward it. To my relief the door was unlocked and opened under my direction. I stepped backward into it for I cared not what lay on the other side; my life was in danger from Fettiplace and his lunatic sister. Moonlight shone through an un-draped window at the rear of the room and bathed the door in silver.

I heard the drawing room door open violently as it was hurled against the frame. "Come out this instant and I may spare you." His voice was savage and base; quite unlike the gentle act he portrayed on our previous encounters.

I stepped backward, away from the door. If he chose to come into the room, my presence would be obvious.

"The lid is open!" I heard Susanna's voice shriek, followed by hysterical weeping.

Steps paced the boards rapidly until, finally content the room was empty, the movement ceased. "Here, take him in your arms, Susanna. Comfort him and kiss his cheek."

I gasped. They were behaving as if the child were alive. I stepped backward again to remove myself from their madness.

"There, there. Be still. Your brother and I are here again."

The room stood before me in a vision of moonlit madness. Fifty corpses, maybe more, stood in silent reverence gazing upon a gallery of faces. All but a few wore no flesh and on those that did, it hung from their skulls like ragged masks. For their final bleak pilgrimage to this hellish church they were dressed in Sunday splendour and stood in perfect order. The focus of their worship was a gallery of the most depraved kind, for every inch of the wall was covered in slaughtered humanity. I walked beside them and gazed upon the faces.

I had been to the carnival and seen the hall of mirrors where I became a beast at the whim of the glass but this was no penny arcade, it was a butcher displaying his wares. I wanted to scream and run from this place, to hide and forget what I had seen, yet the spectacle was so compelling, I could not look away.

What sick amusement could this hold for anyone, save a lunatic and a murderer? At the base of the wall a crude wooden crucifix had been attached, and beside it, in a revered position was yet another face. The face was a decayed and rotting mass, almost unrecognisable as flesh. Dark whiskers jutted forward prominently where the skin had shrunken back.

"Father?" I whispered and stumbled backward. It could not be. It simply could not. I reached out and stroked the whiskers. "Is it you, Father?" I whispered.

My stomach heaved with revulsion and I was forced to look away. But what my eyes fell upon next was far worse a vision.

"Lily?" There was no mistaking my sister's expression. Even after the slaughter, she looked so pretty beside our father. I pulled her face free from the wall and kissed her cheek. "I am sorry Lily. I let you down." My tears fell into her empty sockets and landed on the boards beneath. I took her to the window so I could see her better in the moonlight. "My sweetheart, sister. What have they done to you?"

I felt the burgeoning burn of vengeance scatter amongst my thoughts. As I prepared to let forth a glorious roar, the door creaked open sending me to my knees amongst the congregation.

"Come along, enough of this nonsense. My sister and I are hospitable to one and all, as you can see."

The soft silk of a ladies gown brushed against my cheek. It smelled familiar and sweet, like something from a childhood memory. It held the scent of my mother.

The glow from the lamp crept across the grisly wall, casting shadows across the dead. "Are you sure you closed the lid, Susanna? There is nobody but us here."

"Of course I did! Check the rest of the house at once."

The sound of his footsteps retreated and with them, some of my fear. What horrors lurked in the other rooms in this house? I could not stand to think of it. Instead I took the silken hem of the gown and brought it to my nose. The rotting frame on which it hung wobbled uncertainly in a terrible jig but thankfully remained standing. In amongst this disgusting ensemble I had found a semblance of a lost memory, of a time long ago when my family was whole. When I was content, when my mother still lived.

For how long I remained with that scrap of material in one hand and Lily in the other, I do not know. I sank deeper and deeper into that beautiful reverie, further than I had allowed myself before. It was blissful and there were no corpses or skeletons poisoning the air. There was simply my mother and father and Lily and me.

I must have slept, for the grey light of dawn scratched at the window and pinched my face. With the breaking of the day came the full realisation of whom I had slumbered with. Slack jawed with gaping eye sockets, they stared soullessly at me as if I were one of Booth's lantern shows.

I had to get out and leave this waking nightmare behind. Regardless of my method of entry, I would have to bring the police. This abattoir was something they needed to see. I crept to the door and opened it a little. The candles had been extinguished and the coffin removed. Had she taken the corpse to her room as a mother takes a newborn baby? There was no time to consider what reason lay behind this monstrous arrangement; that would come later. For now I needed to remain undetected and be away.

Every step of my feet brought with it a fresh surge of terror as the boards creaked and the house complained of my presence. Yet before long I stepped into the fresh chill air of the winter morn. I leapt down the steps and onto the street where a lamplighter was going about his business.

"Morning, sir." he uttered and tapped on the windows with his pole as he passed. I hurried away taking one last look over my shoulder. For a moment I thought I saw a face at the attic window. Pallid and ghostlike it vanished with my next step. It may well have been one more of their grisly collection, or Fettiplace himself. I cared not at all, for my heart was filled with relief to be outside once more and with my blessed prize.

The Police

To go home and sleep would be unthinkable, and as I walked the streets in the fresh air of the early morning, I began to wonder if it had been some terrible nightmare. What I had seen was akin to the imaginary horror of a Drury Lane show, not reality. Was I nothing more than a lunatic, bound for the white tiled walls of Bethlem? It would be of no surprise if that were the case, my mind was a wreck.

Would Booth know what to do? It was unlikely; he was ill equipped to deal with anything more serious than his magic lantern or a bottle of port. If I were to go to the police I would be locked up for burglary or declared a madman and thrown into Bethlem. I walked aimlessly waiting for something to happen, for a cab to end my life under wheel or hoof. Would the Lord, upon whom believers placed such reverence, send me guidance?

"Mr Napier, you look dreadful! Come in this instant," John Collins ushered me inside, "I must ask you something, sir. Although I cannot smell gin about you, are you in drink?"

In my usual spirits I might have bristled at such a question but I was simply too weary to react. "No, Mr Collins. Although my mind shares a state of ruin akin to that caused by drink. Is Anna, Miss Collins awake yet?"

"She is taking breakfast upstairs in our apartments. I shall tell her you wish to speak with her."

He led me along the dark corridor into the garish parlour. "If you would care to take a seat?" He indicated the chaise but I took one of the hard chairs instead. He disappeared through a door in the corner of the room.

A few moments passed in uncomfortable silence. It was not a place I felt relaxed, particularly following recent events.

"Matthew?" Anna came into the room and brightened my mood immediately. "John was right, you look terrible. What on earth has happened to make you look so wretched?"

She was so pretty and kind. I could not burden her or John with my terrible discovery. I rose from the chair. "I'm sorry, Anna. I should never have come."

She placed her hand on mine. "From the moment I saw you, Matthew, I knew I was sent to help you. I do not how, and I do not know why, but I will not go against that instinct; it has served me well these years."

"I am plagued with an insidious lunacy, Anna. It creates terrible visions of things which cannot be real. They simply cannot exist for if they did then I am in hell. Just last night…" I could not say what I had seen for who would believe it.

"What happened, Matthew? What has happened since I saw you last?"

I fell to my knees. "There were babies and bones. I saw cadavers praying to the cross in a blasphemous church. My mother was there, Anna; dressed in a silken gown and I slept beside her." I drew my hands down my unshaven face. "It cannot be real! Why am I being tortured so? Why!"

I felt her arm around my shoulder. "Allow me to help you. Allow us both to help you."

The same strong hands that had lifted me from the gutter, hoisted me to my feet. "You shall come upstairs and rest."

Once again I was taken from my misery by John Collins and delivered into salvation. Like a Crimean invalid, I was discharged to bed, and as my shoes and overcoat were removed, I felt the full weight of my grief bear down on my soul. The tears flowed in a silent torrent and soaked the pillow beside my cheek.

"Bring me a chair, John, so I may watch over him."

I lay there until my tears dried and my mind crept free from its tormented cell. Still, Anna remained at my side, watching and whispering softly into my ears.

"Lily loves you. She is safe with your mother. She is happy but she is afraid for you and wants you to be careful."

It was an ordeal to open my eyes for the shame I felt at having wept so openly in front of Anna. She looked down on me; there was no sign of pity or embarrassment, simply kindness. It had been a long time since I had been looked upon in that way.

"You were restless, Matthew. Tossing and turning and calling out for Lily."

I smiled up at her; it felt like an age since I had felt that happy compulsion. "I am sorry for my behaviour. I can assure you, it is quite out of character."

Her expression turned grave. "Please do not apologise. All I ask is that you tell me what it was that disturbed you so. You made little sense in your torpor."

"I cannot, and will not say, for you already think me deranged."

She placed her hand on my cheek. "I do not think you deranged, Matthew. I think you have seen and felt too much without a hand to guide you."

I took her hand and lightly kissed her palm. "I shall tell you but it is truly despicable. Would you hand me my overcoat, please?

I withdrew the butchered face of my sister and held it for Anna to see. She covered her eyes and called for her brother.

John arrived and listened while I regaled them with the truth of what I had seen. As I spoke the words and recalled the images, it seemed like they were some other person's memories and not my own.

I started with the experience from my childhood before moving onto the previous evening's events. When I had gone through the entire story, I waited for a reaction. To my own ears it sounded absurd, so what would they make of it?

Anna spoke first. "I have witnessed things about Louis and Susanna which are troubling. They seem to revel in the anguish of others. She calls it the truth but to me it is spite. Have you not seen it too, John?"

He took her hand as I had often taken Lily's. "If you feel troubled by them, sister, then so do I. You have always felt things that I do not understand but you have always kept the word of the Lord in your heart. Your intentions are without question. I will help you, however I can."

I would never have chance to say such things to my own sister and tears welled in my eyes.

"What must we do? I am ready to be taken to the police if that is what we decide is best. They cannot ignore the evidence."

"We must discuss this carefully, Matthew. We must expose them and bring the full weight of the law upon them. There is also something else we must consider." Anna spoke slowly, choosing her words carefully.

"That being?" I asked.

"We must set those poor spirits free."

I looked down at Lily's face. "We must return them to the earth. Where they all belong." I looked up again, "How long have they been part of this church?" I asked of John.

"They came as soon as I made it known we were here. I took it as a sign because her skills in communing with the dead delivered us a great congregation and without that my work in the community would be impossible. You, Mathew might have perished in the gutter if it weren't for the money they raised."

"And what do they get in return? From what I see they are not God fearing individuals with an altruistic bent." My mind was at last beginning to apply logic to the situation.

Anna jumped in. "They both obtain great pleasure from observing the pain and distress Susanna's lies impart."

"Yes and a good deal of wealth from private consultations." John said blandly.

I rose from the bed. "We shall go to Bloomsbury and find the police station. It shall be done tonight."

*

As we rattled along in the cab, I could not help but question myself again. What if all I had seen were just illusions in a demented mind? Yet, buried deep in my pocket, beside the memento mori of my father, was the macabre mask of my sister's face. I did not need to touch it again to know how real it was.

Three constables and a sergeant were spared to visit the address. The Inspector obviously considered my companions orderlies from the asylum and me a lunatic. I could not bear to show him my sister for I knew he would have taken it from me and now I had her again, I would not let go. Nevertheless he could ignore my pleas for only so long before my insistence bore a dividend.

"Sergeant Shaw, you shall take Mr Napier and his comrades to thirty-four Bedford place and you shall search it top to bottom. If it is, as Mr Napier suggests, a house of horrors, then no doubt half of Leman Street station will be here within minutes to help us."

Sergeant Shaw was a burly man but I feared for him as he entered the unlocked address with his revolver pointing the way.

"Police!" he yawped into the darkness and turned to face us. "You three wait here until I call for you."

We waited as they searched the house. The only sounds came from the muffled laughter of passengers as they passed us in a cab. What was taking them so long? The horrors inside were obvious to anyone.

The sound of gunshot smashed through my imaginings and hurtled me back inside. "Sergeant?" I bounded up the stairs. All my fear had departed, leaving behind a terrible anger.

There was laughter then, terrible raucous laughter.

"Sergeant Shaw!" I threw back the parlour door. The infant's coffin remained, alone and unwelcome in the centre of the room. I did not need to see inside to know it was empty.

"Mr Napier, will you step in here for a moment, please?" Sergeant Shaw stood in the doorway to hell and beckoned me inside.

I did not wish ever to enter that hellish church again yet I knew I must. I must see what Fettiplace had left for me.

The room was empty; the congregation had left. The silent prayers of the deceased would not be answered tonight.

"I do not understand, sergeant. I was not mistaken. I saw…" He stared blankly back.

"The gunshot and the laughter? What caused you to open fire?"

Sergeant Shaw took my shoulders and turned me to face the door. "This. I nearly shot a dead man, which caused a good deal of mirth from my men."

Beside the door, in the piercing light of the moon, was the shrunken mask of a dead man. Below it, in charcoal lines as fine as a spiders legs, was the perfect portrait of me.

"That's you int it, Mister Napier? Don't know who the other poor bugger is though."

"My father." I answered.

*

"I fail to see how they could have moved so many cadavers, so quickly, without drawing attention to the act." I lit the fire and motioned for Anna and John to sit.

———

"A man can move a great many things without notice if he so chooses and has the right connections." John replied.

"Perhaps I was mistaken. I could…"

"Do not say that, Matthew. You were not mistaken as well you know it." Anna remained standing beside me.

"I should say they intend to kill me. By physical or other means I do not know, and for what insane reason, I cannot say. I do not believe I have ever caused them ill."

"I think it is the last we shall see of them. They have had their fun and now they will move on to another victim. If not, the police will capture them and they will surely hang. You are lucky you possess the strength to resist them. I am not sure I could, if I had seen those I love in that room " John stared into the fire.

"I am not sure they will move on until they have their prize." The mantel clock chimed the eleventh hour. "Would you both remain here tonight? I should feel better for all of us if we remain together."

"We shall be happy to." Anna replied.

"Thank you. Anna, you may take my room and John will you take my uncle's room?"

"And where will you sleep?" Anna asked.

"I shall not sleep tonight. I will be quite comfortable here beside the fire, I assure you."

With Anna and John both in bed I took my place beside the fire with a bottle of brandy. There, I withdrew the greater part of my family from the deep dark lining of my pocket. Sergeant Shaw had no use for the wizened flap of flesh my father had become, and so before Anna or John arrived in the room, I took it for myself.

I laid them carefully in my lap, side by side. "See how your daughter has grown, father. She is quite beautiful, is she not?" Their cold, dead flesh was warmed in the glow of the fire and the flames sent glorious shadows to dance on their faces. In my eyes, they were once again, animate and living.

"We need only Mother to be complete again." I kissed my sister's cheek, "It is lovely to have you home again, Lily. Perhaps tomorrow we will take a walk to Drury Lane and see the bearded lady."

Once again the golden abyss which lay within the bottle, consumed my conscious body.

*

As I floated helplessly upward through the various stages of waking, I became aware of a cold, biting ache building through my body. I had not intended to sleep, but with the aid of brandy and the curious warmth emanating from my father and sister, I had drifted off.

The fire had gone out but the morning had not yet broken. It was a miserable time of night when the darkness wraps a velvet cloak about you and takes a sickle to your senses.

I reached down to feel the reassurance from my father and sister but could feel nothing except the cold wool of my trousers. "Lily? Father? Where have you gone?" I reached beneath my legs but my fingers felt only a threadbare patch on the rug. Had I taken them somewhere in my stupor? I would certainly have disturbed Anna had I taken them to my room. Besides, it was something I would recall, and I did not.

I stumbled from the chair and walked across the room. A faint light slid along the banister and pooled at the foot of the stairs. Perhaps Anna and John were also awake; it would not be a surprise in the circumstances. Had one of them come down to me and taken them from me? Why would they do such a thing? I felt anger building in my drunken mind.

Candlelight seeped from beneath their doors, and although my languid mind reminded me of Anna's naked form, I could not enter her room with her brother so close.

I knocked lightly on the door which had once belonged to my mother and father and then to my uncle.

"John, are you awake?" I whispered. His form lay motionless on the bed.

He lay fully clothed on top of the blankets. They had not been used since my uncle's death and were, no doubt, dusty and damp.

Why did his face look so much in shadow? Something was wrong with him. He was at rest as an undertaker would lay a freshly dead corpse for viewing.

"John?" I stepped closer to the bed.

He was dressed in my father's suit, and as the flames danced in the draft, they lit the whiskers upon his face.

"You are not my father!" I leapt onto the bed and took his throat in my hands. "You cannot have him!" I squeezed his throat with all my might and felt the brittle bones in his neck give under my pressure. He was as helpless as a child under my grip and uttered no sound as I choked the life from his body.

When, at last my strength failed, I looked down on what I had wrought. John Collins was dead, undoubtedly, and his ruddy flesh crept around the edges of my father's blackened face creating a duplicitous visage of death.

I had killed a man. I had killed a man whose only crime had been to try and help me. I peeled the leathery countenance from his face and held it to my own.

"Father? Why did you not stop me?"

I must find Anna and explain my actions. I must try to bring order to this madness.

The light from her room, convulsed as if repelled at what it had witnessed. I pushed the door and stepped into the room. "Anna, I can bear it no longer, my mind is destroyed. I have killed John. You must help me."

Her form was as her brother's had been, clothed and ready for the coffin. In my darkest thoughts I knew what to expect, but as I looked down, I saw not the face of Anna Collins, but the shrivelled face of my sister. I felt no rage, only grief for what I must do.

I slid onto the bed beside Anna and caressed her cheek. Her bosom swelled with each breath and her hair fell in gentle curls around my sister's face.

"You cannot have my sister, Anna. She belongs to me." I cupped her neck and pushed my thumbs against her throat. "I am sorry." I whispered. Unlike John, her body trembled and shook as she tried to gain her breath, until slowly she stopped and I released my hold.

"Bravo! What a performance, sir!" The sound of applause broke the pestilent air.

"Now look what you've done, Louis. He's gone and stopped. What about the bleedin' encore?" I looked over my shoulder. Fettiplace and his sister stood in the doorway. Susanna held the skeleton infant to her bosom.

"We shall just have to create one of our own, that's all." Fettiplace came toward me and bought a cudgel down on my head.

Séance of the Souls

I awoke in the parlour, bound to a chair. Around the same table at which we had conducted the séance, sat poor Anna and John. Their bodies slumped forward yet the masks of my family remained.

"Kiss the baby?" Susanna held the skeleton infant before me and pressed the cold bones to my lips. I turned away.

"That's no way to treat your little brother, Matthew. Now kiss him like you mean it."

"My brother?" I whispered.

Louis laughed so hard he doubled over. "Yes, your brother. Although, for an infant, he has been a little quiet of late, wouldn't you say Susanna?"

"He's as lively as the day he was born. Don't you listen to him, Matthew."

"How could he..?"

"Did our father not tell you of his other family, brother? Oh yes, you have a larger family than you thought. Of course your poor mother found it quite unpalatable when she discovered his adulterous nature. It turned her quite mad you know, quite, quite, suicidal actually. Perhaps you feel the same way too? We can but hope."

"No! You are lying to me. Everything you say is a poisonous lie, both of you!" I roared.

He raised his arm and struck me across the face. "Lily was quite the talented locket maker wasn't she? She fought us you know? For such a young girl she had such spirit and for me it was a strange experience, killing a sibling like that. Quite invigorating." He turned his head with a pompous flourish, providing me with his bloated silhouette, "Can you not see the family resemblance?"

"You are nothing but murderous creatures. I am nothing like you."

"Oh come, Matthew," he swept his arm across the table, "Have you not murdered two people tonight? Although one was already dead, but you were not to know that when you did for him."

I looked at John. The fight had left his body before I had my hands around his throat. He had not taken my father's face; I knew this now. I looked to poor Anna; my sister's face drooped from her as she lolled forward. "What have I done?"

"You mustn't take all the plaudits. We've put a lot of effort into this too." Susanna spoke cheerfully and looked down at the baby.

"Why are you doing this to me? I have done nothing to you." I felt the last of my resistance slip quietly away.

"Oh but you have. You have done everything to us. Our father created us and then he deserted us for you. You had everything while we had nothing, except a dying mother and empty bellies." Warm and bitter gin vapours washed over me from his breath.

"No! This is all a lie!" I wept.

"We have our darling sister, Lily present. Our father, Susanna and me of course, yet one person is missing." He drummed his fingers upon my head, "Who can it be? Ah yes, your mother! However can we bring her here to see her family united again? I know! Susanna! Take your place at the table and we will conduct one of your renowned séances. How about that, Matthew? All of you together again, won't that be splendid?"

Reality and nightmare collided with terrible violence, driving shards of agonising torture into my soul. Without the need of surgical instruments, Fettiplace and his sister were performing a lobotomy with excruciating efficiency. My father was an adulterer and I was being punished for his sins, as had my mother and sister. I only wished my punishment would come swiftly and without pain.

Susanna took her place on the table and placed the infant beside her. A single flame illuminated her evil face. "What a shame; we may have to forgo the linking of hands tonight." She closed her eyes, "We are seeking, Emily. Come Emily and communicate with us."

I fought against my bonds. I would have two more souls on my conscience tonight before my mind collapsed entirely and I did not care where this would convey my own.

This time Susanna made no attempt to conceal her deceit and took something from her skirts. It was no larger than her hand but she placed it on her face and spoke. "Matthew, my poor Matthew. Can you see me? It is your mother. They will not grant me passage for I committed a mortal sin and now I am trapped."

Louis howled with laughter. "This is marvellous! What fun!"

The blackened lump of flesh on her face could well have been a piece of cowhide but I knew it was not; I knew exactly who it was.

"Will you not address me, son? Perhaps you are disconcerted by the news of your new family? I was too, so much that I took a razor to my wrists." She leaned back and screamed, "I see that lecherous creature is seated beside me." Susanna struck John, knocking his head to the side. "He should be confined to the pits of hell for what he did to me; to all of you."

"I dare say I should my dear." John turned his head and stroked the whiskers on my father's face.

I retched and felt the hot acid in my mouth. This man had died under the brutal grip of my hands a few moments before.

"Oh come on Mother, you're being far too harsh on him." Anna stood and took her position beside Susanna; my sister's face had slipped to the side revealing Anna's sneer beneath.

The room spun in a terrible carousel as my father joined the rest of my family in tormenting me.

"No…I murdered you both…it cannot be…" My words came in short spasms as my lungs fell empty.

"Matthew, you have neither the strength nor the resolve to take a life. I am so sorry; I have been rude. We all have. Allow me to introduce, Anna and John Fettiplace, your brother and sister. What fine actors they have been! I am sure a career on the stage would be most appropriate. Your father, as you can see, was quite the busy man around town. Yet he had no time for any of us, deciding instead to leave us in the gutter. His affection for you and your sister, however, was limitless, apparently. We are here to witness the demise of his prized possession and that is you. I am sure somewhere he is watching us, completely powerless to do anything to help you. Oh, what drama!"

They all broke into raucous laughter and danced before me as if they were in a dancing saloon. My arms and legs shook uncontrollably and the sourness of long ago consumed brandy erupted from my mouth. I rocked and I rocked.

Soon the laughter diminished and my bonds were untied, yet still I rocked and listened to the sounds of birds in the garden. Lily would be home soon with fresh pastries. She would sing for me again. I rocked.

"I am with you, Matthew," Lily's voice whispered warm and soft into my ear, "I am with you."

The End

You can find out about the author at

Macabrecollection.blogspot.co.uk

or

davidhaynesfiction.weebly.com

And if you feel you would like to leave a review of this collection, simply visit the Amazon page where you purchased the book and follow the instructions.

Thank you for your support.

David Haynes

CPSIA information can be obtained
at www.ICGtesting.com
Printed in the USA
LVOW10s1424240517
535697LV00020B/590/P